4/29/10
To the great Dr. Herbert Jones
From one WRITER to another.
Thanks for the support.
El Espada

The Purple Tigers

El Espada

PublishAmerica
Baltimore

Book cover graphics and photo by Angel Ortez.

ISBN: 1-60836-005-9 (softcover)
ISBN: 978-1-4489-1132-5 (hardcover)
PUBLISHED BY PUBLISHAMERICA, LLLP
www.publishamerica.com
Baltimore

Printed in the United States of America

DEDICATED TO THE MEMORY OF:
Mrs. Juanita Brinkley
And
Mrs. Fannie Delk
Two OUTSTANDING teachers
Who MADE ME BELIEVE that **I am** a writer, (RIP).

ACKNOWLEDGMENTS

IN AMERICA, sports define our heroes, role models, dreams realized and dreams deferred. I have been a zealot and dreamer about sports as a participant and as a fan. But this book is not about me; still, like Sir Gawain in the story of the Green Knight who wore a girdle for protection, I chose to wear fiction.

The original Muse that inspired this story was a teenager who I was privy to mentor. The daughter of a friend of the family I observed her career from the age of fourteen to her blossoming into a professional basketball player with several stints overseas.

Additionally, a bevy of ideas also derived from being a parent and coach to my three sons and their sons Tracy Lavelle, Patrick Dawayne (Patrick Jr.) and Edward Tre' (Timothy Sekou). My drive to encourage and witness athletic prowess extended to my nieces and nephews, Nicole, Nia (lil Sharlie), Sharon, Anthony (Big Pun) and his children Ashley and Anthony Jr., Deconte', Jeremy, Jermaine, Jamal, and Zack. My cousins—Chester, Darrell (Coach D), Arthur (Moon), Omari, James Jr. (J.J.), Justin, and Steve—played an important role. One of my nephews, Garrett, won an Olympic Silver Medal. Observing his commitment, dedication, and pain, I was able to see what it takes to represent this country and achieve world-class athlete status.

But it was Muhammad Ali and Pat Tillman (NFL Arizona Cardinals) who forever shattered my fanaticism for sports. At the height of their professions they gave up sports for very different higher principles. Ali refused to be inducted into the army. Tillman volunteered to be inducted. For his choice he paid the ultimate price. Tillman's unconditional love for his country is an abstract idea I fear that I have forever been robbed from achieving or experiencing in America, because race still matters.

"The words of a talebearer are as wounds, and they go down into the innermost parts of the belly."
Proverbs 26:22

It is a cold winter's night and the wind whispers its weightiness across my features and the faces of the bums in the alleyway where I travel. Fiend eyes steal glances at each other when I bend over to pick up a short tree branch thick enough to club a mugger to his maker. I approach a huddle of desperados around a barrel of campfire light…I throw the wood into the fire. I don't stop to fraternize; still a warm feeling covers my chills as if to say the bums and me are one…one blood…one love.

When I turn the corner, derelicts and other street people mingle around the front of the Greyhound Bus Station while legitimate travelers scurry in and out. Jack the Ripper cross my mind while walking up a dark unlit street. The stench of death bristle my nostril hairs-making me feel so alive. I ain't superstitious; still I notice a black cat cross my path and jump up in the trash bin looking for food. I step over a vagrant stretched out on the ground behind the trash bin trying to sleep off his drunkenness before he becomes a stiff.

My tension eases a little as the change of direction places the wind at my back. Straight ahead, there are young riff-raff standing on the corner laughing and horse playing. As I past the gang—a car stops adjacent to them. One of the group's members goes over and passes dope for dollars on the passenger's side.

As I watch the activity, another one scowls and asks me, "What you looking at old man?"

I know that the only answer the thug would understand is to bust a cap in his ass—I do not reply.

I keep walking; my right hand is itching, not for sure money somewhere in the future, but it is sweating to caress "the bitch." That's what I call the 44 six-shooter that I am strapped with. It does not mean anything, per se, just a term of endearment. I done wore her so long; she done made my shoulder sore. The police have stopped me many times strapped with her. Still, I would rather for them to catch me with her than for young niggaz to catch me without her. The cops don't fuck with me like they did twenty years ago. That's about the only good thing about being black and growing old. Your profile slips under their harassment radar. I don't worry about being patted down when the law stops me. Now, when they stop me all I have to do, usually, is take a neutral stance, pass the eyeball test, and I'm let go.

The sounds of cheering penetrate my senses softly, growing stronger and louder as I make my way through my old neighborhood towards the Carter G. Woodson High School grounds. The Purple Tiger Mascot hanging over the gymnasium's entrance seems like an idol god—my blood begins to boil as I recall memories of glory days gone by. The roar of the crowd lets me know that the spirit of the Purple Tigers is alive and well in the gym as it is in me. I try to attend all of the games—football, basketball and even baseball sometimes. It is my great escape. It relaxes me…high school games, that is, and poetry. I like reading Poe and Blake.

A few blacks are excellent poets and writers, but they use their skills like a license to belly ache about the white man. Give me some shit that rips your guts out like Ai and Wanda Coleman. While in prison, De Sade wrote a novel on shit paper; commitment and dedication, that's what I'm talking about. The poet that awes me, though, ain't Shakespeare; still the irony of it is…he's a hunkie.

Rainer Maria Rilker is a German poet—I ain't really studied his background. He writes with such violet beauty. So passionate, and with a middle name like Maria, he's got to be a sissie—I mean gay. I wonder was he one of those blue-eyed Aryans who thinks that his blood is pure. Regardless, I am a true purple blood through and through—once a Purple Tiger always a Purple Tiger.

~~~

I'm Eddie Jenkins, Sr.—one of the original Purple Tigers. My class, the class of '69, named the mascot and picked the colors. I was a two-sport athlete; played football and basketball for the Purple Tigers. I blew out my knee the last game of the season my senior year hoopin—tore that muscle that connects the knee joints on the side, the anterior cruciate ligament—my ACL. I been a has-been every since. You talking 'bout the jinks—if that wasn't it, a giraffe's pussy ain't high and a bear won't shit in the woods. Back in the day, people didn't know that much about rehabbing sports injuries.

You broke your ass—your ass was through. In fact, my parents' insurance paid for my hospital bills. I think that my dad was reimbursed some of the money—at least the deductible. Anyway, I still get a VIP pass though, I don't have to pay to get in the games—everybody knows me. I prefer to pay, I got a thang about freebies; people always wanting something for nothing. I don't want to be one of those.

Besides, I want to contribute to the program. My record still stands; I hit fifty on their asses. Because I'm quiet most people keep their distance. They think I'm 51-50 because they can't pinpoint me to a job and they see me walking all the time.

That is my exercise. My knee can't stand the pounding that jogging and running place on it. So I like to take long walks to keep my blood flowing. Sometimes I might stretch out my stroll for ten miles. I stay neat and clean, dress conservatively; I try to keep a low profile. I don't need no more attention that I already get.

~~~

Tonight is special for me. The girl's basketball team is playing for the regional championship. If they win, they go to the state. I never looked at girls' basketball seriously, until about four years ago. Yes, that's right, that was when I ran into an old high school flame one day and she told me to come see my baby play ball. I say what baby? She tells me I got a daughter by her. I tell her to get out of here—no such a thing.

Then she was like, "Remember that rainy evening you picked me up at the bus stop…about fourteen maybe fifteen years ago?"

I tell her I remember.

Then she says, "Remember we made love for old time's sake…for the good times… Remember it was a rainy day in April of '81?"

How could I forget? Love didn't have shit to do with it though. I was horny and the bitch was married at the time. All I saw was a big ass waiting at the bus stop. When she got in the car, I was shocked it was Charlene. I used to fuck her when we were in high school when that pussy was young and tender. She was hot as fire. Her mother used to allow her to take her male company in a little sitting room in the house out of plain view from others. I couldn't believe that shit—two teenagers left to abide by what amounted to an honor system.

That day, I swooped down on her like that chivalrous romantic freak, *Don Quixote* or somebody—offered her a ride. She got in and talked small and so forth, but I'm preoccupied with other thoughts. She's talking about how she done got married and goes to church every Sunday and inviting me to come and so forth. I'm full of that cocaine that I've been snorting. I do that after I take care of business sometimes.

Anyway, I'm knowing she a sucker for a hard dick. So, I play on her vanity and ask, "Is that pussy still good as a government check?"

"You better know it, Naw, naw, how them kids say it? You'n know?"

I pulled my pants down while driving and my Johnson is standing like Kareem Abdul Jabbar—tall. I sprinkle some powder on the head and invite her to come and eat it off. "Have some coke and a smile," I say.

Now she's laughing, "Eddie you still crazy."

"Yeah, baby, crazy bout yo big fine ass."

"Boy, take me home to my husband. I don't go back where I already been."

"Sho ya right, but ain't nothing wrong with a little buck naked fun every now and then. Is it? What he don't know can't hurt him." She don't answer. Then I sing, "Lay yo head across my lap and let me feel your warm and tender jibs one more time…like Al Green say, 'For the good times.'"

She's giggling like a silly bitch, now, and then she quiz me like, "What's that you done laced your skeeter wit?"

I told her it was coke. She said she had never did nothing like that. I counter with 'here's a good time to try something new.' I demonstrate how to snort the shit. She's looking at me like I'm crazy as a Bessie Bull, but all the time she dick watching.

After we had rode four or five miles next thing, I know she done snorted the poison up her nose. I sprinkled some more on the same spot, soon she polishing my knob shinier than a hotel housekeeper does. We ended up in one of those hour motel rooms all night long, fucking like we were teenagers again. I ain't seen her since.

I'm half a hundred, she's a couple years younger, and now I'm hearing this shit…nigga please! I ain't going. Regardless, the thought of a daughter kept playing on my mind. I couldn't dismiss it. It wasn't that I was feeling so parental or something, it was the thought of spawning another bastard in this white man's world to be exposed to this *ol' nigger life*.

Twenty-three years ago, I wasted my sperm on a bastard son by another woman. She took me to court, had blood tests, and sent me through the riggamarole to collect child support. What vexed me so was that the woman was making $40,000 a year back then. Plus, I was paying her every week more than what the court ordered me to pay. She didn't care. She just wanted me to stand before that white judge so I could be talked to like a child, 'cause she lied and told the court that she hadn't seen no money from me. I didn't keep no receipts and I paid dearly for that. I ain't religious but I remember reading some where in the Bible about the worst deal in town for any man…is a scorn woman.

Anyway, I played the game until the kid turned eighteen; that bullshit has been over at least five years now. What depresses me so is that my son is a lazy sumbitch. All he wants to do is wear his pants below the crack of his ass, ride around in the car I bought him, blast that fucking rap noise that they call music, smoke weed, drink beer and pretend he's some kind of gangster. He works for me sometimes when he gets broke and can't beg his mammy no more.

One day we were working—some friends of his passed by—the boy fell to the ground as if he was on a battlefield dodging bullets. When I asked what was wrong, you know what the boy told me? Naw, you don't know. Said he can't let his homies see him doing fieldwork, he got an image to protect—nigger's ashame of good honest work. I'm feeling proud about having a business to leave behind for his ass and he is ashamed of it. It's disgusting…here's a nigga with a daddy with his own business and a mammy who's got two master degrees, a decent income and he rejects every opportunity we try to give him for some nigger foolery. You ought to see how he's got that car cut up—niggaration to the highest degree.

Niggers all the time talking 'bout the cops profiling them, hell they profile their own asses. I try not to be too critical; a woman can teach a boy many things, but she can't teach him how to be a man. I can't talk; the fool won't listen to me either. I guess it's some truth to that old cliché, "The fruit don't fall too far from the tree."

Now, I come into the knowledge that I got a bastard bitch; I mean daughter, that's suppose to be mine. I don't know why, but the thought just kept eating at me. You see my good old' God-fearing folks trained me the right way. I made the choice to be what I am.

Charlene's—that's my baby's mamma's name—she's from good stock, too. I heard sometime ago that she's sprung on crack. And, I guess I'm concerned that my suppose-to-be daughter won't be raised properly under those circumstances.

When I saw Charlene at the Exxon pumping gas, I offered to do it for her. She jived me about the last time I faked chivalry—that's when she told me about Carla. She had lost a lot of weight, but she was still frocked to impress. Fashion was always her thing. I remember when we were an item as teenagers, their asses were poorer than Job's turkey, and it didn't have but one feather. She would take those two or three dresses or skirts or whatever, cross match that shit, you'd swear she had a wardrobe Queen Marcos would be envious of.

Yet, I noticed telltale signs, like rotten teeth, repetitive patterns in her speech—kind of slur like—and her movements, they were like fidgety or something. But what really gave her away was that far away look in her eyes. I didn't try to dip or bust her out or nothing, I just listened. All the time she was talking, I'm wondering if I'm the ass hole who turned her out on the shit the last time we were together.

~~~

13

The girls won their game. The boys play next. I sit in the stands watching Carla and her teammates celebrate on their way to the dressing room. A few old heads from back in the day come by to acknowledge me—jocks who wore the purple and black. They know my rap sheet—I was good for 20 points and 10 rebounds on any given night. Some of them lived the legend with me; the night I hit fifty. They come out of respect regardless of the whispers that I've gone crazy.

Niggers are pitiful, I see their moves, they come with praise, but really they're checking to see if they can bury you. Motherfuckers think I'm paranoid—word's out I'm drawing a crazy check. I don't try to refute that nonsense, really I don't mind.

It's to my advantage to let people think what they want. My granddaddy use to say, "It is better to be thought a fool than to open your mouth and remove all doubt."

~~~

After a while, the gym is packed—the crowd roars to its apex when a boy finishes a slam-dunk for the home team. When the teams run to the other end of the court, I make my way down the bleachers and walk behind the Purple Tigers' bench. The head coach recognizes me with dap as I pass. Once out into the hallway, I head toward the concession stand when I notice Carla and some of her teammates standing at the counter. I go unnoticed by Carla as I approach her. Carla asks a student attendant for a hot dog with mustard and a Pepsi. Taking in the exchange of conversation, I listen.

"Carla, how many did you hit tonight?" the attendant asks.

"Twenty-two."

"I heard that," the boy answers, then rushes to fill her order. When he returns, Carla takes her money out to count the cost. However, she's told to forget it because she's got the hook up.

"Everybody loves a star. Everybody wants to pick up the tab for the star lady."

Turning around to see whose talking, Carla sees that it is her mama's old boy friend, me.

"Hey Eddie, did you see me play tonight?"

"Wouldn't have missed it for the world. I didn't see Charlene tonight. Is your mother here?"

"Naw, she wasn't feeling too good. She stayed home in the bed. What did you think of my game?"

Before I answer, I thought about whether I was pissed because Charlene missed such an important game or was I not pleased with Carla's performance. "I don't know what was wrong with you tonight. You looked like you were just floating around out there. You didn't hustle at all."

"I was straight. I was letting the game come to me. I can't do every thang—I hit twenty-two."

"On somebody you should've hit forty. The girl was shorter than you; you were quicker, you should've been stopping and popping all night. You out there fumbling and bumbling."

15

"We won."

"That's good; but when you don't play your best and win, winning is a fraud. You done took your superior talent for granted. Your victory over your opponent's been brought down a notch, 'cause now you have deceived yourself to believe you can win again with the same effort. Understand me? You missed so many open shots. You were like five out of ten from the free-throw line. You passed to people who can't catch, who weren't expecting the ball too many times, and you passed when you should've finished. You made eight assists but you turned the ball over five times. What I tell you about that shit?"

"Know who's out on the floor and what they can do. Keep my turnovers to assists ratio down to one to six or seven assists."

"The only good thing I can say that I like is you created exceptionally well off the dribble and took that rock to the rack with authority when you did go—girl, you played good defense. Still it was like your mind was somewhere else."

"How you figure?"

"Carla, I know you. I know what you capable of doing out there on the court. I know you better than you know yourself. Trust me."

"You don't know me. You think you know me."

"I'm not here to argue. Look....I enjoy watching you play, but my interest in you goes much deeper."

"Why? It ain't like we real kin folks."

"It brings me joy just to watch you play. I want to see you make it big time. I've been through what you're going through and I don't want to see you make the same mistakes I made. When is the last time you smoked weed?"

"At lunch time today."

"At lunch time! On the school grounds?"

"Um huh."

"That's what I'm talking about, indulging in self-defeating bullshit...tricking yourself out of your opportunities. You could have been caught with drugs on school property, there goes a Board suspension, and there goes your reputation among future college coaches. Damn. That explains it…"

"What?"

"Why you were out to lunch on that court."

"Chill out Eddie. It ain't no big deal. My high had wore off way before game time. Besides, I told my friends I wasn't gonna smoke no more if we win tonight 'cause I got to be ready for the state."

"It is a big deal. Them ain't no friends if they offering you dope, especially when they know you playing ball. You can't be putting poison in your body. Your body is your ticket out of this ghetto hellhole. You're an athlete; respect yourself and your body because you and it are special. You can't go out like that. You suppose to be a leader on that team. You need to set a positive example for the others, not just on the court, but off as well. You get comfortable smoking weed; pretty soon you'll be a crack head just like your mammy."

"Fuck you Eddie." She throws the popcorn she's eating in my face, "You don't know shit about my mama neither."

The ruckus caused people to look around at us with astonished faces. Tears are running down Carla's face. She leaves in a hurry with me in pursuit.

"Wait Carla, I didn't mean it like that."

People in the hallway are looking at me as if I am a pervert. My pager vibrates on my hip—I let her go.

A beeper is as high-tech as I ever want to get when it comes to making myself available. I believe that the police are in cahoots with those cell phone companies. Besides tracing every call and message you get, they can pinpoint your exact location. Someone beep me I go to the pay phone and call 'em back. I keep the conversation short and I'm out.

Don't nobody call me unless it's about some money—except for Carla. She calls me all the time, she wants money too, but she tries to get feedback on her game, a ride to and from the beauty shop, help with her homework, real relationship stuff. She puts her code #23—that's her jersey number—in behind the number she's calling from and I generally call her back within ten minutes or less, unless I'm real busy. I generally have to cut her up about her game, but I try to pump her up too. She's a kid that doesn't respond with urgency to positive strokes; she gets the big head too quick. A quick kick in the butt, not literally, but verbally, and she's ready to make you out of a liar. I give her money, but I have to watch myself 'cause I might give her the store, that's how much my feelings have grown for her. I don't know why. I can't see any physical resemblance to me in her, just in her game. She got that from somewhere, that natural talent. I mean she's far more advanced at the stage of her game than when I was that age. I had to work hard to make myself better; she doesn't think she has to. That's what pisses me off more than anything about her.

My son, Eddie Jr., calls me too, when he's broke and needs to work a few days.

I got me a lawn-care business, strictly small time. I don't work for black folks anymore; they too cheap and I don't hire them any more to work for me, either. You see, niggers are some envious impish motherfuckas, they clock riders, no concept of customer service, always whining and complaining "It's too hot, I'm tired," they take unscheduled breaks and all that kind of shit. My money depends on how many yards I can finish in a day.

Niggers carry around saltshakers to drop salt on your name and reputation, just be all up in your business. If I were white, they would have a heat stroke before they ask for a break. The people from the hood—most of them don't even know that I'm enterprising.

Junior, my son, is the only black I let work for me. I got me a Mexican crew; them wetbacks some working motherfuckas and they work cheap, too. I got a Mexican straw boss who speaks English well enough, and I let him handle the business. I don't have to stand around and watch like I have to do my own kind.

However, this number in my beeper now, ain't 'bout no grass cutting. Somebody needs a head cut somewhere. That's my real profession—cutting heads and taking names—some might call me a cutthroat, but it's nothing personal, its just business. I murder people—but only for a fee.

I'm gonna tell you, I don't take every job, especially when it comes to offing niggas. See, there's always a nigga that needs killing, but some niggas be so pitiful they ain't worth killing, at least by me. Understand? I'm good at what I do, and I don't waste my skills just because I can. I told my contact don't come to me with no job where you can get a nigga bumped off for a sack of dope. I been doing this for over 25 years and I ain't been locked up for it, yet. I ain't even been questioned about the bodies I done buried.

That's 'cause I prepare thoroughly before the kill. I studies my targets, their habitat, their habits, everything. I try not to feel one way or another about killing, 'cause, when I let my emotions go, I'd notice I love it too much. It feels like busting a nut sometimes, like you making a power acquisition. You can actually feel yourself taking somebody else's power. You feel like God. When you love your job, success is imminent. I got a Rilke poem I recite after each job, sort of like a ritual. It goes,

"What will you do, God, when I die?
When, I your pitcher, broke, lie?
When, I your drink, go stale or dry
I am your garb, the trade you ply,
You lose your meaning, losing me,
Homeless, without me, you will be
Robbed of your welcome, warm and sweet.
I am your sandals; your tired feet."

I ain't bragging but when I take a job it's a done deal and a clean get away.

~~~

20

What up fool? Yeah, I'm Carla. Carla B. Ware. The B. stands for Billie. That was my grandmama's name—Billie Jean Miller. She died before I was born. Mama made her first name my middle name in her memory. Anyway, I don't much like it, but I respect it for my mama's sake.

Sometimes I can't stand ol' Crazy Eddie. He think he know everything. He be always telling me 'bout my game. To get on his nerve, sometimes I pretend I'm not listening, but I be all ears 'cause it be some good stuff that nigga be telling me. That man is pure. Like one time we went to the gym and he was showing me how to study my shooting form and techniques, how to square up, rotate the ball, keep eyes on the rim and follow through with that wrist action. That man musta hit 20 straight shots without missing one. He shot from all over the place from three-point range, medium range jumpers, off the glass—I mean it was awesome. Then he says, "Think about it, I'm hitting at will and ain't never played college ball, let alone the NBA."

He showed me where I'm really at and where I got to be when it comes to consistency, confidence and shit.

Mama say Eddie was her first real love when she was fifteen. I just turned sixteen last month. Mama never really made it clear to me how come they not still together. She just say sometimes in life you got to move on even if it hurts.

~~~

EDDDIE

When I'm doing contract work, I generally use a 9mn with a silencer for close ups. I keep a German 9mn machine gun strapped on me in case of fire fights, and I have a special made Remington 700 with scope, fold-up stock, and rifling for long distance closings. Depending on the wind speed and direction, using .223 cartridges, I am accurate at 700 yards give or take a few feet. I have closed out deals with Arabs, Armenians, Chinese, and Mexicans, but my contact calls me mostly when a nigga needs killing. It's usually work that the Syndicate don't want to fool with for one reason or another. I don't care, that's more for me. It's quite easy to close on a nigga deal and get away with it, 'cause the police are going to write off nearly every case as gang related or drug deal gone bad. Still, like I said before, I don't waste my skills on no just any nigger.

I learned about weapons when I was drafted in the army back in '72. After I finished AIT, they gave me a medical discharge on account of my knee. In a way that old basketball injury finally paid off because now I got free medical insurance for the rest of my life. I tried to get a disability check based on my medical discharge, but they said the injury was not service connected. While I was in the army, every day I thought about going AWOL. I just wasn't feeling patriotic. With all the racist bullshit I had seen in my short life, I felt like a pure sucker preparing to go to Vietnam for America.

At the same time, I was feeling like a coward if I didn't go. You know, it's funny, sometimes…I feel like a white man trapped in a black man's body.

My grandpa taught me how to shoot long time ago when I was a little boy. We use to hunt rabbit, geese, and quail back in Senatobia, Mississippi. He was a sharecropper, lived in a three-room plantation shack, and in the wintertime, he had to hunt to eat. I remember I was eight years old when he showed me how to hold a shotgun—one of those 12 gauge double-barrels. We went hunting one day. Ol' Roadie, our hunting dog, signaled that something was in the bushes; I locked that thing down on my shoulder, and waited. Moments later that rabbit jumped out of there running for his life with Roadie right behind. I put the gun barrel's sight on that rabbit and fired. That's the last thing I remembered. That thing kicked back so hard, it hit me under the chin and knocked me out cold. When I came to, I was lying in grandpa's bed with a towel of ice on my head and a bandage under my chin.

A couple of days later, grandpa says to me, "Boy you want to go hunting?"

I say, "Yes suh, but, I ain't wanta take no shotgun. Can I take yo pistol?"

He laughed so hard until he cried, that musta've been the funniest shit he'd heard in his life. So, he gave me his pistol, a 44-caliber revolver, great big old thing, so now I'm out there hunting with it stuck in my waist. Whenever Roadie would smoke out game, I'd fire it as if I'm Billie the Kid or pretend I'm fucking Audie Murphy or somebody—wouldn't be hitting jack shit. After I get my shots off, the sound of grandpa's shotgun would send a rabbit rolling like a ball or a bird diving like a kamikaze to its death.

Then grandpa says, "Boy," that was my name to him, he never called me Eddie; "You got to shoot at the spot the rabbit running at. Shoot in front of it; let the bullet meet the rabbit where it's going."

So, I started aiming and shooting at the spot. One day the bullet met the rabbit at the spot. It was as if I could feel butterflies rise in my gut. I walked over to see my work, but now, I don't feel so good. The rabbit is dead. Grandpa see that I'm all choked up inside, tasting my tears against my wishes.

He say, "Boy, a man kill when he have to, that rabbit is food, you got to eat to live."

Grandpa cleaned and pot boiled the rabbit the same as he does all game he kills, still eating the rabbit I killed tasted funny. I ain't like rabbit since, in fact I don't eat meat much anymore—I'm trying to be a vegetarian. It ain't that I'm some kind of health nut, because I till crave meat, and I break my abstinence time after time, it's just that I feel as if I am a cannibal every time I eat it, no matter what kind of flesh it is.

I kept going out there shooting game, but now it was for the dare—to see if I could still do it. I believe that is how I learned to throw the football. I led the Negro Prep League in passing for three straight years. When I chunked that rock, I threw to the spot, that receiver make his cut, that ball be in there on the numbers.

The University of Minnesota recruited me, back in high school, but they wanted me to play defensive back. Said I didn't have the arm strength for that level; shit I could've developed the strength. I said the hell with them. I was going to play basketball for Grambling College, then, I tore my ACL. Those schools fled me as if I was the plague.

I saw my station in life then. I saw that I was just a piece of meat, somebody's meal ticket. Sometimes I think what if I could've rehabbed my injury, walked on somewhere, and let those schools eat off my ass until I could get what I wanted—to play in the league—would I be better off, now,

~~~

CARLA

I'm riding shotgun next to one of the assistant basketball coaches, Vivian Harris. Me, Doc, Gangsta Girl, Caesar, Taffy and Tamika make up the core group of the team. We are going over to Coach Harris's house to spend the weekend. Since we are leaving for the state tournament on Sunday afternoon, the coaches decided that it might be a good idea to keep as many of us together for the weekend to keep us tight and focused. As Coach Harris talks, my mind is elsewhere…

"You guys played a good game tonight. Not perfect, but good. Your turnovers were a little shaky, but they didn't hurt us too bad. The defense was exceptional. Carla, you really harassed the ball tonight—12 steals, that's some kind of record. Everybody's going to have to raise their intensity level up a few notches up there playing those white girls. No offense, Taffy."

"None taken," Taffy replies.

Everybody but me laugh as Coach Harris continues, "They're going to be running plays, coming off screens, setting picks, a whole lot of motion offense. They gonna be in shape."

"We don't care if they be black or white. We in shape too, and we going up there to take care of our business." Caesar adds, "What about it P-Tigers?"

Everybody but me chant, "Purple Tigers, Purple Tigers, holla! Purple Tigers, Purple Tigers, we lead and others—folla! Grrrr!"

Gangsta Girl mocks a cat's meow sound and everybody laughs again except me.

"Why does somebody have to do that silly cat call after every Purple Tiger cheer?" Coach Harris asks.

Tamika responds, "See you don't understand Coach. It's a female thing. See what I'm saying? We wanna be ferocious like P-Tigers and every thing, but, we be like preserving our rights to purr like kittens…letting a nigga think he in charge."

"You mean stay hoochie…" Everybody laughs except me.

"So when we get our freak on—it's all good," Gangsta Girl further explains.

25

"True dat," Tamika concurs.

"You girls are too young for that sort of thing. Get your minds off of sex. Books and ball, that's all you need to be thinking about at this stage of your lives. That's what it's gonna take to make it at the next level, if any of you are expecting to make it in college.

"Coach this is the 90's," Gangsta Girl adds.

I'm *thinking*…See, this the kinda stupid stuff I got to put up with to be on this team. Sex crazy bitches, that's all on they mind. I don't mind though, it can be fun sometimes, I love basketball. Basketball is my life…well, my mama is too. I love my mama more than anything or anyone. Basketball is only a game, but it be like its me. Know what I'm saying? On that court, I be like Jordan— nobody can stop me. I be on fire, I be jacking that thang up from way out there behind the three-point line. I mean sometimes I shoot from half court—just for the hell of it. Coach be mad as hell.

I don't care, he know I be serving that rock like dope on they asses. He say I play like I'm on the playground somewhere, no discipline. But, I just be being me.

Sometimes I just have to take over the game 'cause my teammates be missing and stuff and playing scared like they don't want to shoot when the game be on the line. I ain't scared to shoot it; I want to shoot. I mean I dream about shooting that rock in those kinds of situations. This year I bet I done won four or five games with the last second shot. I ain't scared of nobody, including Coach Dawson. He hollers and cuss me out, make me sit on the bench, but when I'm out there I be seeing things he don't see.

Eddie say trust yourself first—then the system, then your teammates and the coach last, if he worth trusting. Eddie say don't be afraid of change; change your game if something ain't working, change to what the coach says if it is working, don't get stuck in the same mode, and don't be predictable. Coach is alright, when the game is on the line, he wants the ball in my hands. So, I put up with his shit, 'cause we be winning.

Eddie is my man, that's my nigga—he's my mentor. He just came, told me one day, and said that's what he wanted to be to me. I said okay and I told my mama and she said it was okay too, so we been together every since. I told him that people say he crazy. You know what he told me:

"Show me a nigga that says he ain't crazy and I'll show you somebody you better watch night and day 'cause that nigger's crazy."

He makes me laugh 'cause he be saying some funny shit sometimes—and the way he say things—it be off the hook.

Still, he treats me like he cares for me. Makes me read books, and I have to write critiques on 'em. I had never read a whole book before Eddie.

I read *The Bluest Eye* by Toni Morrison, it was boring but it was kinda cool, too. It was about this girl who felt like she was ugly 'cause she didn't have no blue eyes. Her daddy raped her and stuff. Eddie says if I can't read and write well in college, I might as well throw in the towel. He grades me harder than my English teacher does. For every critique I make an A on I get fifty dollars and I get ten dollars for every crossword puzzle. I turn them in ten at a time—that way it looks like I'm banked up—that's a Benjamin, baby. I have read five books and I haven't been able to get but one fifty-dollar pay-off. I'm seeing that it helps because I'm learning new words, and I can see how writing helps you think, you know what I'm saying?

Eddie always correcting my English when I talk, he says that I'm too street-ish, too masculine, talk too much like a nigga. He thinks that I should act more like a lady. But that ain't me. I like my swag. That girlie stuff is weak. 'Cause I like to sag my pants, that don't mean I'm gay. I told my mama what Eddie said about being masculine, she says don't worry what people think…mama trust me.

My daddy know about my mentor, too. I tell him Eddie's like a big brother. I think that he's kind of jealous of Eddie, but he pretends not to be. My daddy gives me money every week of school and I get a dollar for every point I hit in a game. That's why when I lace up, I gots to put up at least twenty. I gots to git paid. I am averaging nineteen points a game, but it's hard 'cause playing point guard, scoring ain't, or rather, isn't my primary role. Coach be wanting me to run the team—that means create openings for others to score.

Another thing Eddie be saying is for me to get serious about, is my schoolwork and my game will take care of itself. All the teachers know I play basketball.

I really don't have to get my lesson, but I do most of the time. Sometimes I get one of those smart bookworm girls to throw something together for me. Them teachers know I don't be writing like that, using them big words, they still give me a good grade. My old history teacher, Mr. Anderson, tried to be hard, but I let Coach Dawson handle him. Coach went and talked to him and he passed me anyway, even though my average was 66 in his class.

Now, my teammates, them my dogs, man. We do almost everything together. Me and Tamika probably the closest. She crazy, but she's levelheaded, too. She keeps me out of trouble. She be always plotting how to get some boy. I like boys, too, but I don't trust them. All they want is to get yo stuff and then they go on to the next fool. I ain't giving up Billie, that's what I call my coochie, to just anybody. I named it after my grandmamma, 'cause it's precious to me. Tamika had sex last year with a boy who she had a crush on—the next day it seemed liked the whole school knew about it. They was calling her a chicken-head ho and everything. She came crying to me. I told her that's all right I still loved her and we been tight every since.

Caesar…she real religious. She says our prayers before games and she always reading the Bible. She ain't that good but she got good fundamentals, works real hard and she gets them stick backs and garbage points every time she gets some minutes.

G.G. that's Gangsta Girl, she got mad skills and she reckless. I have to watch her, she be done stole my shine. She go with this nigga in a gang. I believe she in it too, but she won't admit it. I seen her throwing gang signs and she got tattoos on her neck and booty. But I ain't mad at her. I don't care. Whatever, she in or do, I know she got my back on and off the court.

Doc and Taffy they be tripping. Doc's got great hands when it comes to catching my passes and she can finish down low. Taffy's just a spot up shooter; she can hit the three at times when she's hot. They off the chain. They gay, Doc is suppose to be the man in their relationship. She and Taffy…Taffy's biracial; they be telling me about what they be doing to each other.

Doc be talking bout, "I ate my baby's cha cha good last night…Didn't I?" Right in front of me—

Then Taffy say something like, "I rimmed your booty first."

Then they'll laugh…they so silly, I mean they buck. I don't know whether they be doing all that stuff, but Doc showed me some rubber dildos; some had some straps you fasten around your waist. Doc says when Taffy's been a bad girl; all she gets is dildos up her ass. But when she been sweet, she let Taffy eat the hell outa her pussy.

I asked her if she eat Taffy's pussy, too. She said sometimes when she feel like it, but she say the thang is to get yo nut, if a bitch cum while you fucking her, all well and good, but she don't get off eating no ho's pussy. She be calling herself educating me on them kind of thangs' cause she thinks, I'm gay.

But, I ain't gay. At least I don't think so. I'm strictly dickly, even though I ain't never had one. I'm a virgin. I done seen a lot of skeeters though…skeeters that what my mama call boys' privates. She's from the country. Me and my mama talk about anything; we close like that. Anyway, what was I talking about? Oh, yes!

Boys be showing me their lizards trying to show how big they are…they generally run in three sizes, small, medium and whoppers.

It be funny…the way they be begging and lying trying to get in yo draws. I get urges to be with boys sometimes, but like I told you, I don't trust them…I don't want to be used.

I have to 'fess up and tell you, though, a lot of girls have hit on me and told me that they liked me and stuff. I think it's 'cause I'm a star on the basketball court. One girl stuck a four-page letter in my locker talking 'bout what she would like to do to me. It felt kinda funny reading it, I mean I was like…I don't know how to describe how I felt, but I did feel my pussy get wet.

My mama told me that if someone wannabe nice to you let 'em. She just say know your limits and let them know what they are—'cause people always want something when they do something for you. One time, I saw my mama on her knees begging a man not to leave her. That was after she and my daddy had broke up. I was about seven or eight years old. That's why I got to be strong for her and let her know that we'll always have each other no matter what. I know one thing; I don't ever want to be that weak for no boy or no man.

I did kiss that girl, you know, the same one that wrote that letter. One evening, Coach canceled practice and I was bored and I knew mama wouldn't be home from work when I got there and that girl had been on me 'bout kicking it with her after school, so I invited her over. I was curious, too, about the mess she'd been talking. So, this girl, her name is Tasha, she was like younger than me…no, wait a minute, no she wasn't we were the same age. She was a grade behind. I'm in the eleventh grade and she's in the tenth. Anyway, when we get there, at my house, I'm like in the bathroom peeing. She bursts in on me while I'm sitting on the toilet and went to kissing and sucking all on my neck.

All the while, she's doing it, she spitting game.

"Be what you is Boo…fuck what these niggaz and bitches say…you gay dog. These niggaz ain't giving you shit. Can't nobody love you like I do," and all that kinda stuff.

I'm already up on the moves she bringing, so I say,

"Wait a minute, dog, you don't know me. What's up wit ya?"

She still ain't trying to hear me, the bitch is clamped down on my neck like a vampire and it's feeling kinda good, then I was feeling kinda funny about it, too.

I say, "Girl, get out of here, it ain't even like that dog." At the same time, I'm trying to wipe my coochie. Then when I stand up, she jams her tongue down my throat. So, I did the same thing back to her.

Then she say, "Let me eat yo pussy."

I say, "You nasty; I just got through using the bathroom."

She say she don't care, why should I. I told her I was a virgin and I ain't never had sex.

She shot back, "You'll still be a virgin. It's only when you let a boy penetrate you that you lose your virginity."

Then I think about what my mama say about gay people. She says you can go to hell for that kinda stuff. So, I pushed her back off me and told her to go home. Man, she was bugging, but it wasn't even that critical.

~~~

EDDIE

It seems to me sometimes that the killing fields were my destiny. Though I'm the one making the kills, I still feel that I'm the one down on the killing floor. I didn't ask to be a killer. It was heaped on me…by, by, naw I ain't gonna tell ya.

You might think I'm crazy…a psychopath or something. Okay, I will tell you anyway. See, I use to sell dope-cocaine. I started off selling a little bit to support my habit. The shit was nose candy to me. I had never had more than a couple of ounces to work, but I worked it good, built a loyal clientele and thangs. My supplier was slow so much and a lot of times he couldn't meet my demands in a timely manner.

So, one day I decided to just up and go down to Florida…Miami. Didn't know nothing bout nothing or nobody. Just had heard about these Jamaicans who was suppose to be slanging big time weight. I'm down in there cold canvassing with fifteen G's to cop a kilo. After a couple of weeks, word soon got around about me—that I was somebody looking to score.

This Jamaican…I can't even remember his name, he hooked up with me and we clubbed and kicked it with the fly girls and thangs for a few days. All the while, he's selling me on the notion that he's the-go-between to the dope man. I generally can read people, especially a nigga, I figure he was no cop so I rolled the dice with him and set up a meeting place and time to make the exchange.

I booked two rooms next to each other in a motel. After a short wait, I get a call from him that the party had arrived in the other room and that I was invited over. I tell him to send the one carrying the weight to my room. I wasn't gonna walk into no trap with my money.

Seconds later, this sucker come over, I pat him down; he clean; but he only got an eight ball—talking about he wasn't bringing the keys over until I show him the money. I flashed the cash; he called over next door and tell his people everything checks out.

I'm a hunter. I can read the signs. I got my 44 in my shoulder holster. I know a cross when I see one coming. I know there will be a knock on the door or the door's gonna be knocked open. My gut feelings tell me the latter. So, I pulled *the bitch* up, placed it upside their point man's head and make him lie down on the floor and tell him if he makes one false move or sound it would be his last. I'm standing on the side of the door in the far corner. Moving the window curtain just a crack to scope the situation, I see what's up.

Sure enough, I'm out numbered—four fuckin jackels at my door. Two of 'em carrying what look like one of those ram-charging steel logs the cops use to bust your door down with. The other two, they each got a Mac 10. Boom! The door rips open and the two with the Macs start spraying the place before they even see me. I pick 'em off like sitting ducks…two single headshots. One of the ramshackers raised his gun from his belt to take aim at me; I popped him under his armpit and the other in the upper torso before he could bring his shit out. My slugs like to sent 'em both through the wall they so powerful. That's the beauty of it sometimes…when you meet adversaries head on and come out on top. The rage, the rush…so magnificent, so powerful.

You try to plan for it; but when the shit hit the fan, you're not prepared for it all. You can't pay for that kind of high. Anyway, I still got two shots left. I stand over the Jamaican lying on the floor. He done punked totally, begging for his life, crying, and talking 'bout he didn't know nothing 'bout nothing. But my *bitch* do not play. Now, I'm looking at five dead niggas around me with one bullet left.

As I'm reloading, I walk outside on the balcony headed to sweep out the adjacent room. Before I could get there, the Rasta' Mon who set up the deal burst out the door picking 'em up and laying 'em down. I flipped the cylinder back in place with three bullets, take aim and fire at the spot. Like a rabbit, he runs to meet it.

The impact causes the bag he's carrying to fly like an eagle and tumbles him like desert weeds; only thing different is he's rolling in the parking lot. The shit happens like slow motion—bizarre would be a better way to describe it, 'cause I'm in a zone. In a strange way, it was like it was meant to happen that way. That kind of straight shooting only happens in the movies, with me its real life.

I check their bodies and took off 'bout eight grand between them and hurried to the parking lot to check the bag's contents—kilo of coke, *a workman is worthy of his hire*; I think. I have no emotion about none of it until I walk towards the rolling tumbling target and see that he was still alive. I could hear the police sirens approaching from a distance, but I don't give a fuck. I'm mad at myself now, 'cause I didn't make a clean kill like I did with the others. I put the *bitch* behind his ear and that bullet tear half of his face off.

That's when that *separator* first appeared. Its fog shaped like a human being…got wings…got red eyes beaming like lasers. It took its hand that looks like an eagle's claw and pulled dude's soul right out from his body. Then it perks its lips up like a fag and throw a feint kiss at me and then it kisses the soul of the Rasta mon.

I believe I saw the Angel and the Kiss of Death at the same time. Now, I know there's life after this one. Every time I fulfill a contract, I look for it. Most times, though, I don't have the time to wait and see if it will appear.

~~~

CARLA

My body says go to bed; my mind says finish this crossword puzzle. I'm stalled on filling the spaces for a word that describes a "boxing combo." I give up trying to figure it out myself and ask does anybody know what this is.

Caesar comes over to assist and I tell her its number 12 across. After scratching her head for a hot minute, she says, "That might be something down Doc's alley. Why don't you ask her?"

Doc is in the fridge trying to put something together to feed her face. She comes out from the kitchen with a six-inch French bun stuffed with cold cuts trying to talk with a stuffed mouth. "Did I hear my name mentioned?" Pretending to be shadow boxing, she says, "One, two…How many spaces is it?"

Caesar tells her six spaces.

That's it I say, I tell Doc, "I believe you may be right."

"Sho I'm right." Mimicking Muhammad Ali, she continues, "I am the greatest, I shook the world, I'm a baaaad man…naw, I'm a baaad bitch."

"You got lucky," I say.

"Luck don't got nothing to do with it. I got skills."

"Yeah right."

"Don't hate, appreciate, try to duplicate."

Taffy is shifting through Coach's CD music selection…mostly old school. She asks everybody which one to put on—Marvin Gaye or the Mad Lads. There's a divided response, three for Marvin and two for the Mad Lads even though nobody's ever heard of them. Everybody's tripping on the singing group's name. They suggest that a coin be flipped. Then Taffy asks me because I don't say one way or the other. I tell them to put on Yanni. Everybody laughs.

Someone in the groups hollers, "We ain't ready to go to sleep."

"I got Lil' Kim's *Hardcore* in my backpack." Tamika says.

"Yeah, that bitch be bumping," G.G. adds. "Listening to that ho makes me horny."

"Girl you stay hot for that thug. That nigga got you sprung," Doc ribs G.G.

"Yeah, I'm down for my nig. You ain't mad is ya?"

"A nigga can't do shit for me but give me some money. You better ask somebody." Doc counters.

"Coach will run us out of here if you put that on," Taffy says.

I tell them that I will run their whorish asses out of here if they put Lil' Kim on 'cause I'm trying to concentrate.

"Must we refer to ourselves as bitches and whores? No wonder our boys don't respect us," Caesar interjects.

I'm still wrecking my brain with the crossword puzzle. "Here's one," I say. "Addict…I don't know whether they mean, 'ad'ikt' or 'a-dikt'. My dog, Tamika, catches only the last pronunciation.

She responds, "A dick! Who dick?"

The girls fall out laughing. I tell her not that kind.

"That's the only kind I want," G.G. adds.

"True," someone else says.

"Oooooooooooowee, Y'all so nasty," Taffy jokes.

Still trying to explain the word, "No like you sprung or something," I say.

"Junkie," Caesar replies.

"There's not but four spaces," I answer.

"What kind of dick do you like Reverend Caesar?" Doc asks.

"The Bible forbids fornication. Our bodies are God's temple; and we should treat them as such," Caesar counters.

Doc tells Caesar that she's seen her walking around the school grounds holding hands with Maurice Arnold—a card-carrying nerd. Then she says, "I bet Maurice is trying to put some dick in that temple. Ain't he?"

G.G. like to die laughing. She finally gains her composure and says, "I'm going to call my Boo behind that. Doc, you know you wrong for that."

~~~

EDDIE

"**Mister** please don't shoot me," the fine young fox pleads to me. I motion with my finger to my mouth for her to keep quiet. She's scared shitless because I got the *bitch* in the ready position as I search the room for someone possibly hiding in this sleazy motel. I look in the closet, the bathroom, under the bed, and then I search the dresser drawers for hidden weapons. These days you can't be too careful. These young bitches will set your old lusting ass up to be robbed not just of your money, but your life.

When it comes to sex, I buys it. I been this way every since that bitch I use to go with dropped a dime on me to the police that I was selling drugs. I was good to that woman. Bought her anything she wanted. She wanted more than I could give. She wanted my nuts…I couldn't give 'em to her—no more than letting her oil 'em from time to time. When I set the ceiling for our relationship, the bitch got ignorant; I tried to phase her out easy, but she wouldn't let me. I had to pistol whup that ho like she was a nigga in the street. That's when she broke real bad. I beat the case; cost me plenty, though. After that, I took what money I had left bought me a truck, a lawnmower, weed eater supplies and started a lawn care business. It was a hand to mouth operation for a few years, now it sustains itself—in fact I got more business than I can comfortably handle. I got two trucks, two trailers, four riding mowers, blowers and just a whole lot of other equipment. That's another story—back to the issue at hand.

I usually don't go out into the streets looking for no ho. Ain't nothing out there but crack head strawberries and cops pretending to be hoes running those reverse sting operations to catch Johns. I go across the state line, get me a hotel room at one of the casinos, then I sit at the bar and I get all the action I want. I don't discuss prices, the bitch might be the police, but I let a woman know that if she is about her business, she's gonna be treated like a professional. See, I ain't no trick, per se, a real ho knows the difference between a trick and a business man who just wants to contract her services.

For what I want, a good ho would be satisfied with $50 or less. When I'm done with whatever, I break 'em off at least a c-note for trusting the process. Hoes be trying to give me their phone numbers and trying to sleep over. I ain't trying to hear that shit. These days, all a bitch can do for me is crawl her larceny-hearted ass in, do the business, and crawl her stanky ass back out until next time, if there be a next time.

But tonight is different. This pretty young strumpet I picked up on the bricks is fresh…she's too young to be a cop. She couldn't be more than seventeen if that. Probably just got turned out by some low-life pimp. I may be her first real trick. Once she sees that all I want to do is secure the place for my safety, she relaxes and eagerly provides her public services without asking for her money up front. I could have left without paying her and she would have been happy just to be still alive.

I ain't no Samarian but I got scruples. Like I said before, I ain't looking for no freebies and that includes a free knob slopping, and besides the young bitch needs a career defining experience. I tell her before I leave if she's going to make it in this game, she better not show any fear to a customer no matter what, 'cause everybody ain't gonna be as nice as me.

~~~

CARLA

Back at the sleepover, Doc tells Taffy to roll her a blunt. She says to all of us, "I got some Indo, yall."

I try to discourage that idea, "We need to chill off of that. Every team up there's gonna be tough. We need every edge we can get to beat 'em."

Taffy stalls her movement to go get Doc's bag, when Doc goes off on her.

"Bitch, do like I tell you." Then she addresses me.

"Ho, you better stay up out of mine. What's up wit you? You know you the main nigga be chiefing like a chimney. Quit flaggin."

"Don't be calling me outa my name. I ain't no ho." I tell her.

"Whatever," she says.

I take a deep breathe to calm the rage I feel inside, then I tell everybody that I promised somebody that I would stop getting high and be an example to my teammates from here on out.

"Well, I ain't promised nobody shit. You ain't got to hit it."

Caesar tells Doc that she has already been suspended from the team once before.

"Suspended! You got me fucked up. I quit, dog. Coach Dawson didn't suspend me. Motherfucker ain't qualified to suspend me."

In spite of my anger towards her, I ask Doc what happened to make her quit. She told me on the down low that Coach Dawson exposed himself to her while they were alone in his office one day. So, I say, "For real? Man quit lying."

"I swear that on everything I love," Doc says. Then she adds, "I wouldn't put that out on nobody if it wasn't true. I ain't no angel, but I ain't that kinda nigga, dog."

"What happened? Why you ain't tell nobody?"

"I told him I was going to tell the principal. The man broke down and cried. Have you ever seen a grown man break down and cry?"

I shake my head no.

I'm talking 'bout the man bawled like he was a bitch.

Mocking the head coach, Doc goes into her act, "'Please don't destroy me. Think about my wife and children. They need me to take care of them, I'll do anything you ask. I'm sorry, D.J., I thought you wanted it. I misread you. It's my fault. Please forgive me.'"

"So, I tell him, I got to think about it. I told him I couldn't play for him no more, though. He said that he understood and then he kept on begging me to promise him I wouldn't tell it. I finally felt sorry for him and gave my word that I wouldn't—and I didn't tell...not until what I told you just then.

"Sometimes I wished I had. I had that man's life in the palm of my hands. That shit he did fucked with my head for a long time...still do sometimes. These coaches be talking 'bout character building and work ethics, and all that other bullshit and all the time be figuring out how they can get in your panties. That's the reason I don't give a fuck no more. These folks ain't real. It's whatever, whatever; know what I'm saying?

"The only reason I came back is because he came to me. Told me he didn't want me to miss out on any scholarship opportunities my last year. Said, I could go upper majors D-1 with my skills and shit like that. So, I thought the nigga may be right, so I came back. The man been giving me money and shit every since. I tell him I want to go to the mall...he ask me how much you need?"

I'm shocked like a big dog 'bout Doc's story, but I'm still curious about something, so I ask, "How big was it?"

We both laugh at my question and then Doc says, "I couldn't tell with his wrinkled up ass shit. If I had wanted to fuck...that nigger's dick was a complete turn off. Talking 'bout, 'How you like this?'"

I like to died laughing at the thought of tough-talking Coach Dawson with a wrinkled up skeeter. That shit was hilarious.

~~~

EDDIE

I finally landed a good yard contract with an Italian Mafioso—Tony Santos, was his name. The guy is a few years younger than me. I thought he was a CEO or something. Anyhow, he try to pull rank on the sly…requesting that I come to his back door whenever I need to conduct business with him. I see the man's got an ego problem but I don't sweat it. I play along with him, 'cause he's paying me enough to pay a crew and cover my whole overhead on several other jobs and still make a profit. I knew he was into something heavy or he was just a paranoid Diego because of all the surveillance cameras and equipment…chauffeurs and shit.

Mr. Santos, that's what I call him, even though now he's ask me to just call him Tony. But, addressing him as Mr., helps keep my distance and besides my mother use to say, "It don't hurt to be polite." Anyway, he lives in this gated mansion with his wife and three kids. One day, early in the morning, I go by there to get my money. We got an agreement that I'm paid in cash. Don't send me no check in the mail. I don't want no paper trail.

Alright…I'm at the back door waiting to be let into the kitchen when the sun reflects off of something into my eyes just as he's opening the door. I look up and see a helicopter with someone in its door taking dead aim with a rifle at him or me. I push my way in the door—at the same time I took Mr. Santos down to the floor just before the bullet come crashing into the window. Moments later the chopper lowers almost to ground level spitting out gunfire like an army cavalry bird.

Mr. Santos on the floor now, scared to death shaking…like someone with epilepsy. I ask what the fuck is going on. He say somebody's trying to kill him. Really, that's obvious I can see. I ask did he have a gun in the house. He told me in the den and the bedroom. I had to literally drag his ass to show me where the guns were. I copped a Beretta 16 shot 9mm, a World War II Japanese automatic pistol and then we run to his bedroom.

Mrs. Santos is holding a baby, damn near naked, pussy hairs, titties and every other carnal knowledge showing. Me, the yard nigger, is privy to all this. She's screaming about the other kids in their bedroom and trying to make her way to them. I grab her and hold her until Mr. Santos can restrain her as we all hit the floor. After we calm Mrs. Santos somewhat, I make her promise that she'd stay down for her baby's sake, and then order her husband to crawl to the kids' bedroom with me. He follows me through the gunfire, shattering glass, and furniture flying everywhere.

When we get to the kids' bedroom, both of them are crying, one of them has been shot and is bleeding like a killing hog. I see that he's hit in his right shoulder. I rip a bed sheet into pieces and tie a strip tight at his pressure point on his arm muscle. Another piece I apply directly to the wound and tell Mr. Santos to keep pressure on it. I tell him and the kids to stay put. My radar tells me that people have entered the house to search and kill anything living. I take a deep breathe and go out into rooms firing at anything that moves. When the smoke clears, five assassins lay dead in the Santos' mansion—all from my desperation, marksmanship and manifest destiny.

I go tell Mr. And Mrs. Santos they can come out now. He tells his wife to put pressure on their son's wound, and then we both walk around the house to survey and access the casualties. He puts back on his bigwig hat and tells me that I got talent and should be doing bigger things than cutting yards. He tells me not to worry about a thing, to leave and wait until I hear from him. He would take care of his son getting medical treatment, the wet work, and any police inquiries and things. I looked through him like the shattered glass on the floor unfretted by none of what had happened, and told him I would leave as soon as he pay me my money for the lawn services that he owed me for.

~~~

CARLA

G.G.'s on her cell phone, the girls are still laughing at Doc's jiving of Caesar. I'm still working the puzzle, stuck on the word *addict* when G. G. says, "Y'all, be quiet—I'm trying to talk to my man. I can't hardly hear."

"Go outside, bitch," Doc bellows.

"Fool, don't be calling me outa my name. You don't know me like that. Don't even play, dog."

"My bad, man, it ain't even that crucial."

"God help you Doc. I can't do nothing but pray for you," Caesar adds.

"Does God help you pull those splinters out of your scrubbish ass when you sitting on that bench?"

All the girls laugh at Doc's humor except me and Caesar. I feel like I got to take up for her 'cause she's kinda weak in a way. Know what I'm saying. So, I say, "Why y'all want to bag on Caesar? She brought us through fifteen games and we won all 'em without Doc."

That quieted them for a moment, then Doc walks up to me, she gots to get in the last word, she says, "Well, I'm back now…Suckers to the left…"

Then Doc feints a blow at me and hollers, "Hook!"

On impulse, I throw my arm up to block the blow and grab her in the collar and she grabs me in mine like we gonna jack. The others attempt to pry us apart.

"Carla, chill baby girl, I was just kidding. *Hook* is the word you were trying to figure out for the puzzle. So, I faked a left hook. Why you so up tight, dog?"

Doc is smart like that, she be busting them test out without even studying. I tell her, "You violating…don't be skitzing like that with me. I don't play like that."

Finally, G.G. step in between us. "That ain't no way for Tigers to act," she says. Someone in the background hollers, "What kind of tigers?"

We all go like a chorus, "Purple Tigers, Purple Tigers, holla! Purple Tigers, Purple Tigers, we lead and others…folla!" Everybody gives each other dap and we go back to chillin like nothing never happened. Soon after, G.G. tells me that her nigger, Carlos, better known as Yo Dog is in route. She says something heavy is going down, but she don't say what it is…

~~~

42

EDDIE

After the shootout at the Santos' place, Mr. Santo tried to be my friend, but I don't trust him. I feel like we got something on each other and one of us might not like it to the extent that somebody's got to go and it ain't gonna be me. He tries flattery and tells me that I was Cool Hand Luke under fire. Say, he could use somebody with my talent for more important things.

That's when he offered me this other business opportunity. He tells me he would pay me X amount of dollars to whack somebody—half down and the balance once the job was completed. I thought he was tactless in using that incriminating word, but I don't attempt to correct him outright. Instead, I told him that all monies are payable upfront prior to the objective and if I couldn't name my price we didn't have a deal. We agreed to my position.

I don't like nobody to count my money. But I'm going to tell you. I divide these type jobs into four levels ranging from 10G to a hundred. I quote to my employer what level the job is after I have staked out the target and accessed the degree of difficulty. I don't depend entirely on Tony's or anybody else's information. I shadow the mark myself for however long it takes me to come up with a plan of action. Most of my quarry be sniper action, that's what I prefer, a nice clean take out order.

I do sometimes have to physically confront the subjects to fulfill my purpose. For that, I use a .22 with a silencer, or if I have to fabricate the gang-related thang, I use the 9mm. After I drop 'em I'll turn 'em over and spray their asses with lead...that's a sign of disrespect between the black gangs.

I have collected a level one fee only once. On that occasion, Tony referred me to these corporate stiff-neck types. One thing I learned fucking with this shit, don't let the politeness of a person fool you. Them be the most ruthless snakes you can ever deal with. And white folks are some of the politest people you will ever meet.

Anyway, in the still of the night down by the sea, I met these three people. I'm wearing a ski mask listening as they tell me their problem. They said that they represented the board of directors of a corporation and that the board had decided to take over the company. They needed to get rid of the founder, CEO and majority shareholder. If they killed him, his interest would go to his wife who was anxious to sell the company.

They wanted the wife killed and wanted it to look like her husband did it. That way, when the owner is convicted of murder and sent to prison, the wife would be out the picture and they could take over the business on a moral clause.

That kind of job called for some creative thinking. I told them that I would think about it and get back with them. I took a twenty grand application fee to study the mark's habits and so forth and to cover any unforeseen out-of-pocket expenses. I don't take no job unless I can assure its success. When I accept a job, like I told you, all monies are due prior to; I don't want to hear from the employer again unless there's another job offer. My word is my bond, and that's the guiding principle I work by.

For two weeks, I watched this target. She had no flaws I could take advantage of, no undercover lover, no gambling habits; she didn't even smoke cigarettes—just a rich homemaker trying to live the nice quiet life. She went to church on Sundays, to her bridge club on Tuesdays, seemed to like grocery shopping—had dinner cooked and served for her husband most evenings. From the outside, they seemed to be a happily married middle-aged couple, no children, had their lives in standard Ward/June Cleaver order.

Her husband liked to work in his garage and tinker with antique cars. He prided himself on building them up from scratch and entering them to compete in car shows around the country. That was his relaxation. As I inspected his garage one day, it was here that I spotted an opening. The toughest problem was to find a way to get his blood samples. I am not going into the details how I did that. The game is to be sold not told…understand? Alright, after I accomplished this, I called the man one day and pretended that I was an antique car dealer with a 1932 Chevrolet. I had Kinko's send him pictures over the Internet. He was ready to buy before I could close the deal, but I string him along until I was ready to seal his fate.

Finally, we agreed to meet in Jasper, Alabama on a Monday night. I suggested some places for him to stay and he let me know his itinerary down to the "t."

44

That Monday night was something I'll never forget. On all the other jobs, I was detached like a motherfucker, on this one that woman and me merged as if she was my soul mate. I came in on her like a thief in the night while she was in the den looking at television. I muffed her mouth from behind and told her not to make a sound and don't make a move. At the same time, I slashed her throat from ear to ear…It was over then. I don't know even today, whether that woman's body froze from fear or the beautiful necklace I gave her. She died instantly it seemed. When I came from behind and faced her, her eyes were shocked wide-open.

I stuck my blade in her heart and twisted it—them Bette Davis eyes of hers didn't blink. I'm looking in her face for some life signs—only existence I see is blood draining from her corpse drenching my hands with the guilt of sin. All the time, I'm thinking and talking to myself while I'm sticking her, "Whose gonna save you this time missy? Whose gonna save the day? Whose gonna save your virtue and white purity? The Klu Klux Klan? Where is Mighty Mouse? Popeye the Sailor Man? Where is Superman? Batman? John Wayne? Will Jesus help you? All those hunkified heroes, where they at bitch?"

"Where is Danny Glover? Morgan Freeman? Denzel? Will Smith? And, all them other save the white woman niggas—where they at?" I must to have stuck her over a hundred times…blood gushing like an oil strike from the holes I'm punching into her torso—then that *fog thing* appear.

Only this time, it comes at me and possesses my body like the Loa of Death in the blackest night of a Haitian ritual. I shake so bad that I actually ejaculate. The nut I bust is so violent I faint as if I am a Voodoo slave filled with the spirits of his love gods.

I lay there paralyzed like a zombie—I can't move. My reaction scares the fuck out of me, literally. I ain't lying…I'm there lying still…like a leftover chicken wing on the carpeted floor, blood everywhere, but I can't move—paralyzed. I know I need to but I can't 'cause I'm possessed by a force stronger than life it seems.

You know what I think. I believe what I experienced that night was evil in its most pure form and the scary part is that it felt so good. I wonder why. I don't think that I am a racist or prejudiced or whatever, still I think it was the sweet taste of revenge on a hunkie's ass that made me feel that way. It felt like I was getting back at the white man through his woman like he had gotten to me through mine.

They say a man's got nothing to fear when he loves his job, that success is imminent. I saw that I loved that kill; I was in my element; as if I was a bloodthirsty werewolf. When I finally could move again, I had to will myself from tasting the blood.

I committed a regrettable act—only thing that worries me, it wasn't for my freedom or some noble idea—it was for money. Even today, that money can't soothe the unrest that I feel all the time for slaughtering that innocent woman.

The hits I make, generally, the victims done chose that life, the path of vice, graft, and shit, they had done weighed the risks of the dance with death. They know that sometimes when you dance with that angel; it might be your last. I feel that my hands are dirty, when it comes to that white woman. I feel disdain for myself more than those white-woman saving niggers that I despise.

Maybe, I hate myself, 'cause it seems as if I am in a constant battle with demons in my mind—a conscience is a dangerous liability in this field. So, I tell myself there is no such thing as innocents—collateral damage is how the white folks classify it—either you are a predator or a prey—eat or be eaten. My murder fees are the spoils of war. I get chills every time I try to justify that killing.

You get to cumming from something like that, you soon be a killing fiend, crazy as all get out. You liable be out here stalking women for the thrill of it…and white women at that.

~~~

GANGSTA GIRL

My name is Janice Fuller, better known as Gangsta Girl. My teammates call me G.G. for short. I been ballin' since seventh grade. I'm a Junior now—same as Carla. Me and her been together since Junior High. We use to be best friends but now she be hanging with Tamika real tight. They use to think me and Carla was fucking 'cause we was so thick. We dressed alike, spent the night at each other cribs and thangs. It never ceases to amaze me…how come men can hang out with each other and be best friends, but nobody suggest they are gay. Let girls do the same thing and everybody wanna know what's up with you and whoever. That ain't fair. Since I got tight with my nig, Yo Dog, me and Carla kinda drifted apart. She will always be my dog, though.

I started going with Yo Dog when I was a freshman. He was a senior. I use to see him hanging out at school with them thug niggas and shit. When I walked by all of them except him would be trying to holla at a nigga, but they don't know how to come to a lady. Anyway—Yo Dog made them respect me. The whole thang may have been scripted for all I know; still I was made to feel special.

Not that I couldn't take care of myself, but I guess you can say that I fell for his game. So we been together every since. He respects my hoop game and don't try to take that from me.

I am a real ghetto pearl. Thug shit don't turn me on. My nigga turn me on. It was me who acted a fool and asked to join KFL, *Killas for Life*, Yo Dog's sect. He didn't want me to become a gang member. He tried to tell me that thug life was some real shit. My fass ass gots to be down with my man. Now, that I'm in it, I want out; but there ain't no out…short of death or the penitentiary.

Maybe moving out of town and staying on the down low for the rest of my life might work. For initiation, I got my ass sexed in and secretly I feel like a whore, even though Yo say's that I'm only his. I have been a member over a year now. My mama don't know, but she suspects something. I ain't worried about that—I can handle her.

Coach Harris got a basketball goal in her driveway. I'm weak at free throws, but on the real, I want to be outside when my Boo drives up. I ask Caesar to rebound for me. Doc and Taffy came too; they stand near the sidewalk, passing a joint between them. As they give each other a shotgun, Carla comes out—she's still got that puzzle.

She asks Doc does she know a word that means, "To settle a dispute." She say the word had seven spaces.

Doc can't think of any and then tells Carla to quit trying to blow her high. Carla know better than to ask me. I don't know what's up with her and that puzzle shit. She says it will build her vocabulary and help her get ready for the ACT. I know Carla got game, girl got mad skills, all the top schools be on her jock, but she ain't no college material. She don't study; she likes to party and get high too much. She ain't gonna do nothing but flunk out. She gonna end up right back in the ghetto with the rest of us niggas.

I ain't trying to hate on her or nothing. I just know the truth. The only reason she be doing them puzzles…is 'cause that old man she calls her mentor be giving her money to do 'em. A real student be on they shit case that's them. My mom wants me to go to college. That ain't me. I can't wait to finish high school and get away from her and all of her expectations.

I shoot about a hundred free throws—make about 65 before Yo Dog rolls up in his Lex' sitting on twinkies. When he gets out of the car and comes into the driveway, Doc and Taffy stop their sideshow. I need to speak with him in private. I thank Caesar for chasing down my balls and say to the others, "Can a nigga get a little PT with her man?"

"Sho you right, dog. Let's go." Doc tells Taffy. Then she won't let well enough along, she still trying to be up in mine.

She says to me, "You want a hit of this before I go?"

"Naw, she don't want none," Yo Dog say before I could answer.

"Excuse me," Doc sarcastically responds before she vamps.

"Why you so cold to her, Boo?" I ask.

"I don't want your mouth on nothing that pussy eating bitch's lips been on."

"You didn't have to be rude about it."

"Shit, I wasn't rude. I was direct. Fuck that bitch. She probably dick dyking on the sly. That ain't what I come here to talk about."

"Doc's cool. Don't be so ugly, Boo. You don't have to down people 'cause you don't agree with their life style."

"Whatever…how'd we get on that conversation? You 'bout to make me lose my thoughts defending that…Look, you know that job you did for me last week?"

I nod my head as if to say yes I remember. Our unit jacked one of the Vice Rulers dope houses and I drove the get away car. I never been so scared in my life. But I did it for my nigga. Yo Dog continue talking.

"One of those fools' lookouts got your license tag number as you were driving away. They traced it back to your mama's car. She may be in danger. But, I don't think so. Everybody knows you drive her car. Still I'm worried. They just might hit her to get back at you. I think you ought to stay on the DL until we can answer any retaliation. We may have started a war."

Now I am frightened to death. The thought of *Vice Rulers* killing my mama is unbearable. Yo Dog tells me to try not to worry. He'd keep a still watch near her house for a few weeks. He says if I tell my mama, she won't do nothing but go to the police. He says you got to keep soldier business away from civilians, always. I'm the one who's the target. They know I play basketball and who I play for. My man tells me that I should vanish for a while and not expose myself at the state. I tell him I can't let my teammates down, that I want that championship—I want that ring.

My Boo then brings out this gat from under his jacket and gives it to me. He wants me to be strapped just in case. We hug and kiss and then he leaves for his car. I stop him and ask can we make a block before he goes. He tells me okay and we ride through out town bumping sounds for a while before he brings me back to coach's house.

Once inside, I go into the bathroom and gargle my mouth. When I come out, Doc bag on me with some hateration.

"Girl, you squalling mighy loud up in there. You didn't get nothing caught up in your throat or your teeth, did you?"

Then her lap dog, Taffy, adds insult to injury with, "Like some cum or pubic hairs?" I tell the bitch she don't know who she's fucking with, when Doc comes to her defense and says, "Now, G. ain't no need in you gittin all hostile and shit. We all done sucked dick before."

Carla swears on everything that she loves that she hasn't and never will; says she got too much pride to do something like that. Then Doc says to Carla, "You ain't never sucked one 'cause you got one yo self. You just won't admit it…" Speaking down low under her breathe she continues, "Dyke."

49

"Don't be mumbling nigga, I bet you won't call me that to my face." Carla says. She and Doc face off again.

Tamika saves the scrap when she say to Doc, "Is sex all you ever think about?"

"If God had made anything better, He'd kept it to his self." Doc replies.

"Thou shall not use the Lord thy God's name in vain," Caesar quickly adds.

"Girl, if I hear one more sermon outa you I'mma scream. How come what I say gotta be in vain? Who's to say what I say ain't right?"

"You ain't trying to hide that you gay and you ain't trying to get help. The Bible speaks against homosexuality. Read Leviticus. It also speaks against fornication and stuff like that," Caesar explains.

"Fornication? Define it. I'll do it for you…sex between two unmarried people. It don't single out which sex they are."

I'm curious about what point Doc is trying to make, so I ask, "So what are you saying?"

"The Bible doesn't condemn my lifestyle anymore than it does yours. It forbids the sex act if you're not married. Know what I'm saying? As far as men being gay and shit, that's on them; God made me female, if He made me at all. I may have made Him"

"Blasphemy…girl you going to burn in hell!" Caesar interrupts.

Doc sticks out her chest, makes muscles in her arms, then opens her mouth and pretends that she's screaming out of her head as if she's taunting someone with a celebrated basketball dunk. Everybody laughs at the gesture.

"I ain't no man. If God want to tell me something, speak to me. I ain't got to go through no man to get my messages from God. We are two different sexes, two different lives; don't bunch mine up with any man in a package deal. I'm me. Know what I'm saying. Why am I defending myself to this nerd?"

"Cause you are guilty as sin," Caesar says. Everybody laughs at Doc.

Carla changes the subject. "Somebody give me another word for, "*To settle a dispute*." It's got seven spaces. I got three of the letters, O-U-T, it's something *out*.

~~~

DOC

I am that bad bad bitch…Dorothy Jones is my given name…such a common moniker for a brilliant person. Yea, I like pussy. So what? What's the big deal? I mean, it's the birth canal; all life came through one. That fucking Caesar…all these religious motherfuckers get on my nerve trying to make out like they right and everybody else is wrong.

I read the Bible like anybody else. It's a lot of contradictory shit in there. I could show that Caesar bitch something, but it ain't gonna do no good. Like she talking about that last days stuff and I'm going to burn in hell shit, I'm gonna read them something out of that Bible. Something about two bitches having sex. One of them get caught up in the rapture and one gets left behind.

"Coach Harris, you got a Bible?"

"Sure, what you trying to find out?"

"Oh, nothing, just something I want to read." See, I don't mean to slight Coach Harris, but she's like any other grown person in her generation. They fucked up about same sex relationships and ain't no use in wasting your time trying to make them understand. I am going to turn to Luke the 17th Chapter and read you the 35th and 36th verses. These verses are in red, so that's supposed to be Jesus talking.

It goes, "*I tell you, in that night there shall be two men in one bed; the one shall be taken and the other shall be left.*" The next verse reads, "*Two women shall be grinding together; the one shall be taken, and the other left.*"

What are two men doing in the same bed if they ain't fucking? It makes it clear in the next verse when it talks about two women grinding together. Some say that the grinding that's being referred to is about two women grinding corn or grain of something. But I believe if those hoes ain't bumping pearl tongues, my name ain't what is.

The point I am making is whatever they are doing, one gets taken away and one gets left behind. The ones that are taken away are supposed to be taken somewhere with God. So, it's some good gays and some good lesbians. So, I feel that I got a 50/50 chance of going to heaven just like any other motherfucker. You feel me?

All females be checking each other out. We look at each other butts, compare our hair and skin texture. We be jealous of each others good looks. Them so call straight bitches who be talking about another woman can't do nothing for them…I don't buy that shit. Until you try something, don't knock it. They might not never be with another woman, but I bet you anything, they have thought about it.

My girl, Carla Ware, "Showtime" is what we call her. I like her, Show's game be on. But, I believe she be hating on me sometimes. I know she's gay. She just won't admit it. The bitch plays too much like a man. I wish I could play like that. I ain't seen many boys do the stuff that she does with that rock. That bitch be running thangs…heifer be dishing that thang—making stars out of everybody. I won't tell her though, bitch's head already fat as an Escalade. She cool though, but I swear between her and that preaching bitch…which one is the worse, I don't know.

On the real though, Carla is very popular around school, she cute too, a lot of girls like her—some have come up to me and straight out ask me to hook them up with Carla. Like I said before, she ain't come out the closet, yet. She don't know who she is, I sure would like to be the one that turn her ass out.

Some old fart that she associates with got her all geeked up thinking she world class of something, got her dreaming about playing in the league. She probably could play in the WNBA but she has to make it in college first. There are a lot of Carlas on that level. I will probably go to college, too, if I get a scholarship like Coach thinks. But, right now, I'm just doing me.

Taffy…she's my boo, as much as I hate my name, still I can't help but wonder what kinda bitch would name her daughter, Taffy?

~~~

TAFFY

I am bi-racial. My name is what it is. My father lives in England. He is in British Intelligence. He got my mom pregnant while she was over there studying Shakespearean Theatre for her MFA thesis. Mom is an associate professor at the local university. She tells me that it is best to stay out of my dad's life because he is married and it is less dangerous or something like that. She accepts whatever money he might send for my upkeep, but I think she does not want to make waves for fear of being cut off from her link with British royalty. My father is suppose to be related somewhere down the line to one of the Queens of England. She's always reminding me that I am suppose to be some kind of blue blood, but I ain't trying to hear that shit. She tells me whenever I fill out an application and it asks to identify my race, I should mark the place where it says *other*—that way she says it will allow me to respect both my parents' culture. I use to mark the other but now I make sure I mark African-American or black. I am most proud of my black heritage.

I went to England last summer for a week—stayed in this expensive hotel…ordered anything I wanted. I don't know how much that bill was. My dad came by every day and we went sightseeing, he bought me a lot of things, but he didn't take me to meet his family. I guess I'm suppose to be straight with our little bastardry arrangement because he's white and he's suppose to be some big woo de do. I could care less about that bloody mess. My mom doesn't really like basketball; she hates the school I go to even though I am an honor student. She says I am slumming, when I could be in a white honors program across town. I wanted to go—excuse my Ebonics, where *"the real hooping's at."*

I probably could do a few things with my hair and pass for white if I really wanted to. My nose is straight enough, but I can't get enough of my black side. Mom be too uptight about everything and she's always trying to drill that fake shit into me. I guess I identify with black people so much because they don't give a fuck. It's like whatever, whatever. Mom wanted to act on stage but that didn't pay the bills. She played it safe, got her degree and now she teaches. I don't want to play nothing safe, I want it all. I might not play as well as some of the girls on the team or in our conference, but I am a starter and I can hold my own. I accomplished whatever level I'm at without any encouragement from my mom. If I don't get an athletic scholarship, I am sure to get one for academics, I made 33 on the ACT.

I'm really not gay; I don't even like to think of myself as bi-sexual because I really prefer boys. But niggers be tripping, they all want to be some kind of playa or pimp, this Mac daddy shit is the only way they know how to relate to a female, and that shit gets old…you heard me?

Doc doesn't want to accept my preference and I don't want to hurt her, so I creep to get my freak on with boys. I just like to have fun. I'm not in love with Doc…I've told her that I loved her in the heat of passion, but I do like her a lot though. She ain't fake like some people I know. She is what she is. She's the one who turned me out to experiment with same sex stuff. She spent the weekend at my house once and she made love to my coochie all night long. My shit was so sore the next morning. Doc is jealous of Carla because she thinks I like her.

I don't like Carla like that. I am the team captain but everybody knows she is our leader. Coach Dawson says Carla is a bad example to represent the team as captain because she smokes weed and has this carefree demeanor. She wears do-rags and sags her pants—she the illest and realist person you ever want to meet. I ain't hating on her. I think she's cool people and she catches a lot of flack for just being herself.

One day at practice, Coach Dawson sat on a thumbtack in his favorite chair. He jumped up and hollered so loud, he scared the whole team. The whole team was feeling sorry for him or either snickering real low, but Carla laughed so hard until she cried. Coach was so mad; he accused her of putting the tack in his chair. He made everybody run after practice until we almost died. I started to quit that day. I even started to confirm that Carla did put the tack in his seat. The tack was the same color that she and I had used that day for our science project that we presented to class. I did not say anything about it though. I believe that is our real bond.

~~

54

EDDIE

When the police found that woman's body the next morning and taped the crime scene, I knew they would include the trash bin within the parameters. I had splattered the woman's blood on her husband's mechanic clothes and put them in a plastic bag, with his work gloves, a towel with the husband's blood on it, and the weapon used. For added emphasis, I took the three-carat diamond wedding ring off the woman's finger and placed it in the bag with the other items. That way, it would look like the killer was trying to make it appear like a breaking and entering situation that turned into a robbery and murder. I ransacked a few dresser drawers, threw books on the floor from the bookcase, and tracked up the carpet with size twelve feet in his size ten-work boots. I called the husband and told him his wife was in danger and he called the cops from the hotel he stayed at in Jasper, Alabama. The cops arrived just before the trash was to be picked up and they stopped the sanitation workers from carting it off. When they searched it…bingo!—the plastic bag and its contents. They didn't buy his story that he received a call from somebody who sounded like he was black. The old, classic white man's put-it on-a-nigger-lie did not work this time—mainly because it was true—a nigger did do it. I believe because I made sure the time of death corresponded with the time it took the husband to leave the crime scene and drive to Jasper had something to do with it, too. He was tried and he was convicted.

All the niggas that's been railroaded by white folks and sent up the river to die, I thought I would feel good about this little design, but I don't. Some people I guess, money won't change them. I have always been a good person at heart. I try to con myself into believing that I'm just playing out the cards that life has dealt me. But, when I really reflect on my life, I see that I laid the foundation to be dealt this hand by life.

Like I said before and I'm going to say again…that *fog ghost* appeared after I killed that woman. Why? I don't know; maybe she was a witch in disguise. This time, it hovered over her body and sucked the blood from around her neck, all the while looking up at me, while doing it. I was frozen with fear and trembling inside. It felt as if that thang was sucking my vitals and slopping the semen that I had wasted while sticking that woman.

I told myself it was just my imagination running away with me. Still, that does not stop my nightmares about that time and it don't stop them hellhounds that be on my trail. It does not stop the pain that I live with every day that comes from slaughtering what I believe was an innocent woman.

~~~

TAMIKA

I'm Carla's best friend…at least that's what I tell myself. I know she has four or five best friends. I play guard/forward on the team. Basically, I am a role player. I can hit my shot. Carla set you up so smooth, you be so wide open, you better hit it or Coach going to sit your ass down. And, I don't like to pick splinters. What I like about basketball is that playing this game makes me somebody. I am not just somebody who goes to school, do their work, and stuff. I represent the school. I represent my neighborhood. People treat you different when they know you can do something and represent. Know what I'm saying?

Every since I was in elementary school I have dreamed of wearing the Purple Tigers' colors. At first, I wanted to be a majorette, but then I grew with knock-knees and that was out. I thought about playing in the band; you guessed it…I couldn't play dead. Then I started playing basketball with my brothers instead of watching. At first, I was awful; that ball was so heavy, I use to just throw it up any kind of way. I kept on trying to learn to shoot and dribble; it became a challenge to me. I started liking it. When my brothers started picking me to run with them at the playground, I knew that I had found something that I was good at it. They encouraged me to go out for the team and I made JV my ninth grade year. I made varsity the next year and this year, my junior year I have started every game.

Every since I lost my virginity to an asshole who didn't deserve the time of day from me, I have been celibate. I get urges to do it again but I fight it off. I go and jog a mile or two, or lift weights. My brothers got a weight bench on the back porch. I can bench press over one hundred pounds. Carla teases me; she calls me cock strong.

~~~

CARLA

I got up early the next morning, put on my sweats, running shoes and go to the bathroom to pee. It's locked—Taffy's in there. I tell her to hurry up. When she opens the door minutes later, the air freshner's scent mixed with rotten odor tells me Taffy dropped a bomb. She wants to know where I am going. I tell her that I am running around the neighborhood to get my blood pumping. Taffy asks me to wait for her. She wants to run with me. I tell her I ain't got time. The real reason—I don't want to have to deal with Doc's shit. When I get back, I get the basketball and practice my moves in the driveway. I pretend to be backing down a defender toward the low post. I switch hands from left to right, dip with an up and under and skip to the hole with a sweet finger roll…butter! Taffy comes out the back door dressed in her gear and starts stretching.

"Girl, I couldn't go back to sleep with you bouncing that ball. I might as well get up and join you. I didn't know you get up so early."

"Early bird gets the worm," I say. Then I whip a crisp behind the back pass to her. Even though Taffy is touching her toes, she springs up and catches the ball with Jerry Rice sure hands.

"Let me warm up, girl."

"Good hands, Dog," I tell her.

I continue practicing on my handles. Now, I'm in the triple threat position; moving my body from the pivot, I dribble behind my back, between my legs and do crossover feints. Taffy spots up in the corner and I hit her with a pass— she drains it. I start feeding her passes—she drops five straight baskets before she misses. As I retrieve the rebound, she challenges me to a game of around-the-world.

I pass her the ball and then I ask, "Good as you look; you can have anybody you want to. Why do you let Doc push you around?"

"You don't do so bad yourself. I see all those dudes on your jock…and girls too. How many boyfriends do you have?" I am a little irked by the mention of girls but I don't let on. I only respond to the boyfriend question.

"I got about seven boyfriends, but I ain't talking to about four of 'em."

"What do you mean?"

"Well, I'm not really claiming but four. The others, it's like whatever, whatever."

"See Show, you don't understand. It is like you say. I let her push me around. It's a role, girl. Like playacting. She wants to play the man sort of, so, I kind of let her. Besides…the boys that I want to talk to, seem to be flaky and afraid of me. The ones that talk to me seem like all they want to do is to dog you out. They all want to be pimps and playas. I ain't got time to raise no boys or teach them how to treat a lady. You know what I'm saying? Maybe being bi-racial has something to do with it. I don't know. Doc…she's really sweet. She's just insecure about us."

"What's the difference between letting a nigga push you around and letting a bitch push you around? I don't get it."

"See, Doc can act tuff and all Butch as she wants to in public. But behind closed doors, when she undresses and we are in the bed together, I am the one who gets to see her for what she is. She's just another female with a pussy and we both know it. She probably dick dying on the down low."

I don't say nothing behind that. Meanwhile, while we've been talking, I have left Taffy in the opposite corner and only need to make two shots in a row to win the game. As I prepare to make the first one, Doc comes out into the driveway.

"Y'all could've woke a nigga up if y'all wus gonna be working up a sweat and thangs."

Taffy whines some unclear shit that I don't understand.

I don't answer Doc. I just drain both shots, and say to Taffy, "See ya, wouldn't want to be ya." Then I go in the house to shower.

When I come out the bathroom the house is busy. G.G. is ironing her jeans. The rest of the crew is either packing for the trip or in and out of the two bathrooms washing up or brushing their teeth. Coach Harris is in the kitchen cooking breakfast. I flop on the sofa to relax. Doc eases up beside me and whispers in my ear.

"You know you in violation." I look at her like she's retarded. She continues, "That's my bitch you was with this morning. You got to come through me to fuck with her. That's how you do that there."

"I don't know how come you be tripping, dog. You ain't running nothing—not here. I talk to who I want to when I want to and I ain't got to go through you or nobody else to do it." Doc points her finger in my face and I knock her hand away. Next thing I know, we fighting like cats and dogs, knocking over lamps and any and everything and anybody that gets in the way. Coach Harris is surprised and shocked. She rushes from the kitchen, gets between us, and yells. "Break it up! What the hell is going on in here? Break it up! What's wrong with you two?'

"She first started it. Ask her," I say, pointing at Doc.

"It ain't nothing Coach, just a little misunderstanding. I'm cool." Doc replies.

"Misunderstanding my ass. Y'all are going to pay for everything that's broken in here. Misunderstanding…you two should be able to iron out your differences better that that." Coach say if it happens again, she's going to jump in it and kick both of our asses. Then she make us shake hands. We take it a step further and hug each other.

G.G. is still at the ironing board, she yells aloud, "Iron out! Show, that's it. It's got seven letters, *iron out*, the missing word to the puzzle last night."

~~~

CARLA AT GAME TIME

The Purple Tigers are playing against Bradford County. It is the third quarter and we are down by twelve points. Coach Dawson calls a time out when we get the ball. We huddle up listen to him and catch a blow.

"Y'all slacking on defense…giving up easy shots and lay-ups. You act like we ain't been over this shit in practice. Pick up the intensity. Crunch time—no time to get tired now. Ok, let's get focused. All right, on one. One!"

"DEFENSE!" the team yells. As I'm going back out on the court, Coach calls me back.

"Ware!"

"Sir."

"Shoot the ball. Make some shots. Make something happen."

I passed the ball from out of bounds and I bring it down the court. The girl who is defending me is talking trash trying to play me close. She calls me a hood rat and tells me that I will not make another shot. I drive her to the top of the key, stop and pop a three. The crowd is in frenzies, but I ain't hearing it, I'm 'bout my business. We are down by nine. It' on like a pot of neck bones, now.

I see fire in my teammates eyes; we sprint like horses back to defend our goal. A Bradford player tries to answer with a lay up, but Doc pimp slaps her shit into the hands of Tamika. She turns it into a fast break, the ball touching three players' hands without touching the floor with me finishing it off. We are down by seven.

It is the fourth quarter now; we are still down by seven. The Bradford team is stalling, trying to use up the clock. They bring the ball up the court on every possession slow as possible. They zip passes from corner to corner. While rotating I have studied their scheme and timing. I step into a passing lane and reflect the ball to Tamika. She looks for the fast break but decides to set up a play and pass the ball back to me. My defender talks more smack.

"Bitch, you got lucky the last time." I whip the ball into Doc on the low post. They got two defenders checking her, now. She flips the ball back to me. We play a one-two back and forth game. My defender is still vocalizing, "What you gonna do, bitch? You scared to shoot now?" I make my move to go around her—she slides in front of me and I do my patented spin move to avoid a charge call. Another defender anticipates the move and picks my pocket before I can stop her. She passes the ball to my defender who finishes a lay-up. Frustrated, now, when my defender passes me, I throw a flagrant elbow on her for the world to see and receive a technical foul. Coach Dawson calls a time out. I see smoke coming out of his ears as I approach the bench. "Ware, what the hell do you think you're doing? What did you foul that girl for?"

"She called me a bitch."

"She called you a bitch...Ware, have you lost your god damn mind?"

"No, sir."

"Ware, you lose this game on some bullshit, I'm going to do more than call you a bitch. I'm going to beat your ass like you one. Now, team, let us get back out there and play some ball like you want to win. She called you a bitch. Ware, sit yo ass down on that bench. Caesar get out there. Tamika play the point. On one...one!"

"DEFENSE!"

~~~

CAESAR

My father named me. His name is Arthur Augustas. He wanted a boy. He went to college after he got out of the army. He and my mom never married—they have two children together, my older sister and me. Now mom has six children. My half brothers and sisters got different daddies. My parents grew up in the PV projects as kids. PV stands for Pussy Valley. It got that name because all the girls who lived there were supposed to be fast and easy to have sex with.

I was not one of those girls. I'm not a virgin, either. My cousin use to rape me when I was twelve years old. He was sixteen. He said if I told he would do something real bad to my mama. At first, it use to hurt, when he did it to me. After a while, it started feeling good. I use to hate him so much, but another part of me started to look forward to those rapes. I hate myself for that sometimes. Then I grew tall one summer—taller than him. I started fighting back and one day I actually beat him up. I was fifteen and six feet tall. I told him if he ever touched me again I was going to call the police. He never bothered me again.

Coach Dawson saw me one day at school and told me if I didn't come out for basketball practice, he was going to fail me in Physical Ed. I knew he was just playing, but I came to practice anyway. That's how I got started playing basketball.

When I was a little girl, one day my daddy told me that God called him to preach. I use to sit in his lap and we use to read the Bible together until I was about fourteen; I'm seventeen now. Now days, daddy is not well; now, he preaches to telegram poles. He has a few favorite poles around town where you can find him. He just stands there with his head against the pole, handkerchief in hand and preaches until he's drenched with sweat or gets too hoarse. Sometimes, I stand behind him where he can't see me and listen to him. I have watched him for over an hour. He preaches some good sermons too, better than the preachers in the church do. Mama says drugs did him in. I'm not sure about that. He loved mama; but she wouldn't stop sleeping around.

I still go to church, but not like I use to. If you have Jesus in your heart, I believe that the church is inside of you. I know the Bible tell you not to forsake your assembly. But, people are so fake in the church. I also go to some of daddy's hangouts to talk to him and let him know that I still love him. When I have it, I give him money. Sometimes we sit at McDonald's and talk about life and the Bible. He really knows his Bible.

Sometimes, I think I am a big hypocrite though, because I let Arnold put his hands under my dress. Jesus said all things are made new through him. I believe that I am renewed every time I ask for his forgiveness. If it wasn't for my faith, I might be crazy, too.

Basketball is my escape from PV. I don't have to go home to our crowded apartment after school so soon. The team eats free at school, on the road; we have fund raising activities, and the game is fun and good exercise. Mama weighs over three hundred pounds. I'm big boned like she is and I guard against ballooning up like that. Basketball helps me do that. A couple of Junior Colleges are recruiting me. Only thing I don't like about basketball are the shorts that you have to wear. I don't like how my legs look. I think the uniforms at times expose too much. I wish we wore long pants like in the warm-ups.

I'm surprised to be out here on the floor with the game on the line. Usually, I get in when Dorothy gets in foul trouble or we are blowing somebody out. I got to play tough now. We can win this game. I wish Carla was out here on the floor. She will keep me straight, let me know when I'm out of place and then drop a dime when I am open. If I can just out rebound Dorothy while I'm out here, I'll feel alright when Coach sits me back down. I can't stand her. I better pray, "Lord, please forgive me for being so prideful. Direct my footsteps for your glory." I get an offensive rebound and put it back up for two points. We are down by eight points.

~~~

CARLA

I am mad at myself more than anybody. How did I let that bitch rattle me like that? There are five minutes left in the game. I pray, "Lord, please let Coach put me back in." I try to think of something else to say, "I'm sorry for being unsportsmanlike."

I hear Coach call my name and I dash up to him. He tells me to check back in. Our next possession, I'm back out there on the court running thangs. I drive to the corner and drain a trey. Now, we down by five. We hold them to one shot because Doc snatches the rebound like Dennis Rodman streaking butt-naked.

In our transition, I spot Taffy in her favorite spot on the wing and dish the rock to her. She pay me back with a back door assist; I'm fouled, I make my free-throw. We down by two. There are twenty-five seconds left in the game. Bradford calls for a timed out.

When we get to our bench, Coach Lawson pauses for a moment, he stares me in the eyes like he got a problem then says, "Listen up. Their coach is probably telling them to take care of the ball. They know we are going to press. They've been breaking our press all night. We got to get that ball by any means necessary. Taffy, guard their best ball handler; number 24. You and Tamika double on her."

I know without question, Coach wants to free me up to come up with something.

When the ball is signaled in play, we show press. When they make the inbound pass, we hurry back into our defense down court. The ball handler walks her way up the court.

I'm on the opposite side of the court from her. I leave the player I'm guarding and come around on her blindside, knock the ball loose and race to the other end of the court with an easy lay-up in sight.

Tonight the referees have been stingy with the calls in our favor and Bradford has a foul to give. One of their players grabs me from behind, the whistle blows, and I can't shoot free throws to tie the game. Coach Dawson calls a final time out. He is really fired up now.

"That's what I'm talking bout! The game's over. Even though we still down by two—It's over. But, they ain't gonna give it to you. You got to take it, just like you did that ball when you were on defense. Ok, here's the play. Run the zipper pin-down sideline out-of-bounds play. Get the ball to Ware. Ok, win—on one. One!"

"SHOWTIME!"

Coach Dawson is caught by surprise about our new break battle cry. But, it's something we had talked about among ourselves and we said we would do it, if ever there were seconds in the game with me the designated shooter. Coach likes to keep it simple and let us run and gun at will. But sometimes, he comes up with some pretty complicated shit. This play we are about to execute is some real pro-type shit we run through in practice sometimes.

I line up in a double stack with the center, Doc, on the opposite side of the floor from where the ball is being thrown in. Tamika plays the point. She and Taffy line up the same way on the other side of the lane. G.G. inbounds the ball. Doc and Taffy set picks on me and Tamika's defenders, freeing us up for a moment, but the ball is coming to me. When I get it, the others spread out leaving me alone to work one-on-one with the trash talker. She's on me like glue, steady talking her bitch this and bitch that shit.

I check the clock; make sure I am behind the three point line—nine seconds left. I think of MJ… I dribble with my left hand slowly, reverse the ball behind my neck to my right hand as I break to the right quickly. My defender breaks with me turning her back slightly to keep up. I take my left hand and shove her on, stop on the dime, square up and follow through with my patent jump shot.

The momentum that I gave my defender takes her out of range and she can't get back to contest my shot effectively. Nothing but net. I stand there like the Stature of Liberty with my wrist still bent savoring this dream. I am so into the moment, I don't see my teammates coming. They rush me and knock me to the floor. I'm at the bottom of the pile, now crying, lost somewhere in my own thoughts. We have won and advance to the championship game.

In the locker room everybody's celebrating, patting each other's asses, crying tears of joy, high and low fiving, making cat calls…

Coach Dawson enters. "Listen up. I'm proud of you all. You pulled it off big-time. You think that game was tough. Well, it don't get any easier. Nobody's giving us nothing. The referees are against us, the crowd…we ain't got nobody but ourselves. If you want it, you got to take it.

Enjoy your celebration. You earned it. Make it short-lived. The clock's still ticking for who's going to show up to play in the championship game. I want that state title. But I can't play the game for you. You got to play it. Get your rest and get back focused. Ware, the press wants to interview you."

~~~

EDDIE

I didn't go to Carla's game at the state tournament; I had pressing matters I had to attend to locally. I'm glued to the radio. A small watt radio station with ties to the public school system broadcasted the game using high school students as announcers. They did a great job, gave Carla accolades all throughout the game. Bob Costas and Stewart Scott better watch their backs. I am beaming with pride, over come with joy—it is strange…indescribable—when you can see your life unfold through a child's—it's something like an epiphany.

I stare at my desk and a letter opener on top of an envelope. Tears running down my face blur my eyes. The envelope came in the mail today and dares me to open it. It contains the DNA results from Carla's and my blood and saliva samples. I really want to know if she's my daughter. Three weeks ago, I encouraged her to go with me to a DNA testing site under the ruse that we were going to check our heritage background to determine what African tribe we most likely originated. I am not sure I want to know the truth. I am not sure I can handle it. I tell myself that I might jinx the Purple Tigers' chances to victory if I open the envelope prior to the championship game, so the truth remains under the scaffold.

~~~

CARLA

Me, Tamika, Doc, Taffy, and G.G. go shopping at the mall on our day off. Tamika wants to get a tattoo-a rose with thorns on her ass for all niggas to kiss—she says. Then she comes up with this weird idea. "I was thinking…What if we all went into the championship game tomorrow night with our faces painted purple and black like our colors. We would scare the shit out of them bitches."

I tell her she's crazy—Coach would make our asses run all the way home down the highway. Doc thinks it's cool. Dennis Rodman paints his hair, ass and no telling what else she reasons. "There's no rule against it. We would make a statement they'd never forget."

"What if we lost? We would be the clowns of the century," G.G. says.

"Lost! Sheeeit. That word ain't even in my vocabulary. I ain't no Indian, I don't need no paint on my face to go to war…my game's gonna be on," I say.

Doc tells me that I am always spoiling the fun. She compromises and proposes that we buy the paint to see how we look with it on our faces just for the fun of it. They agree to do it, when they come and watch the NBA game between Indiana and Philadelphia in our room tonight…I'm rooming with G.G. Reggie Miller and Allen Iverson are my favorite players. If I had a choice to have sex with either one, it would be a hard choice. I would have to have both of them niggas. Reggie so fine and A.I. so real, I just don't know.

Later in the hotel room, I knock on the bathroom door before I come in and startle G.G. who is looking in the mirror at herself. She seemed to be agonized as I zip in and sit on the toilet—as Eddie would say, "to make water." I ask her to excuse me for breaking in on her and tell her that I had to use it. I also tell her that she looks like she got the heebee jeebees and ask her what's wrong.

"Am I that obvious?" She says.

"You acting all paranoid, like you done stole something."

Slowly G.G. pulls a gun out from under her jersey. I'm scared shitless. I feel like I might get in trouble. When I ask her what's with the gun she says…

"Don't bug out on me, Show. I got to keep it for protection until this shit blows over."

69

I want to know what shit is she talking about. She tells me that she is afraid for her mother. Then goes into something about jacking some drugs off of one of the Vice Rulers' dope boys that she had something to do with. Me with my crazy self, I want to hold the gun. I have never held a real gun before. G.G. let me hold it for a moment. I stand and point it at myself in the mirror, G.G. tells me, "Give it back; it ain't nothing to play with. Don't tell the others, please. You are the only one I can trust. I needed to talk to somebody. I can't focus thinking about my mama."

"If I were you, I would warn my mama. Tell her to go stay some where else for awhile."

G.G. tells me if she told she would be violating the KFL's code against discussing business with outsiders. She's also afraid her mother will go to the police and everyone will know that she has talked. I tell her she has a choice, to be true to Yo Dog or true to her mama. "If I thought my mama was in danger from some shit I've done, the thought of not telling her would not cross my mind. I'd take my chances with whatever's coming to me." Then I feel around on the gun. I feel powerful.

"Don't touch that! That's the safety. I'll take you target shooting one day, but not now. Just chill and hand it back." G.G. ejects the clip, empties 16 bullets and puts it back in. Then she show me how to slide the barrel back and cock the 9mm and get it ready for firing. She say when you fire, the empty shells come out and it automatically put another bullet in the chamber to fire. It sound so complicated, yet it sound so cool.

After G.G. reloads the gun, a knock comes on the door. We hurry and stash it under my bed and open the door for Doc, Taffy, and Tamika. Caesar comes a few minutes later to everybody's surprise. We all gather around Tamika at the mirror excited and laughing. When she gets through painting her face, Tamika looks like a Zulu warrior. Taffy gets into the act, she trims her colors with white but the white paint don't stand out next against her light skin, so we suggest that her colors be trimmed with red. Somebody's lipstick does the trick. Doc makes her face up like the Cat Woman. I finally give in and paint one side of my face as if I'm wearing a mask like the Phantom of the Opera. G.G. tells us that she can't think of nothing to do with her face. She says that we have taken all the good designs. I tell her to put some stripes around her face like a jungle soldier.

"That might work," She says. I'm going to get me a soda. I'll check it out when I get back."

COACH DAWSON

I'm head coach for the girl's basketball team at Carter G. Woodson High School. I'm also the Athletic Director. I have been coaching basketball in some capacity for about twenty years. I've been head coach for the girl's basketball team nearly fifteen years. In all my coaching tenure I have never coached a player as talented as Ware. The other side of the coin is that I have never coached a hard-headed insolent player boy or girl as that bitch; Ware. That girl don't know who she fucking with!

Showtime...Ware, she, put her teammates up to pulling that monkeyshine shit on me. If I didn't want to win that state championship so bad, that bitch wouldn't dress out tomorrow night. I ain't lying either. I can put with a lot of nonsense from kids, but disrespect, I can't tolerate. I can't run my team with an outlaw bitch like Ware. A player got to know who they play for to get the maximum production out of their skills. Girls oome here every year wanting to try out for what they believe is the school's team. Bitch, you play for me!

~~~

CARLA

Minutes later when a knock comes on the door, I tell Tamika to let G.G. in. When Tamika opens the door, a young man standing at the door surprises her. Her painted face startles him. From under his coat, he pulls out a machinegun and starts shooting at everybody. We all screaming and running like crazy. Blood splashing all over the walls, I try to run into the bathroom, but Doc beats me and locks the door. I feel my knee give out and fall to the floor. A bullet went through the back of my leg and came out through my kneecap.

Somehow, I crawled under the bed next to G.G.'s pistol. Without thinking about it, I released the safety, pulled back the chamber, roll out from under the bed and start firing at any man I see. One of the niggers I hit in the stomach. He falls back against the wall and he screams, "The bitch done shot me!"

Then another nigger came in shooting and grabbed the nigga I hit and they both run down the hall to the elevator. Somebody must have been holding the elevator doors open because they went straight down and didn't have to wait. Next thing I know, the police are pointing guns at me telling me to drop it or they will shoot. I try to tell them that I've been hit, as well as, a couple of other girls—they ain't trying to hear that. Drop it or they will shoot is the last thing I remember before I pass out.

~~~

THE CRIME SCENE

In the middle of medic ambulances, fire department vehicles, TV mobile units and crowds of people along with the remaining members of the basketball team huddle up outside to stay warm, while authorities check out the scene. A newscaster holding a mike in front of the motel speaks to the camera.

"This is Channel 3 news reporter, Ned Johnson, on the scene of what appears to be a bizarre tragedy involving a shooting of a high school girls' basketball team. In a life resembling art theatre drama, the scene looked like a shootout between followers of Charles Manson and Marilyn Manson. It is believed that three or four young male blacks who wore hoods ambushed the girls. We don't have all the facts, but sources say that there is one confirmed dead, and two wounded—one critical. All the victims had their faces painted like some satanic ritual. The police are on the scene putting the pieces together. The shooting is believed to be gang related. All the victims are players of the Carter G. Woodson girls' basketball team who are in the Capitol city from…

CARLA'S LIVING ROOM

As the newscaster continues, Carla' mother happens to be watching the local news. She is terrified that her daughter may be hurt in the shooting.

Her mind flashes back eight years ago, with her and Carla sitting in a movie theatre eating popcorn and watching the movie *Coal Miner's Daughter*. A scene on the screen shows where the star was once white trash poor. She recalls Carla asking her, "Mama, are we poor like that?"

"Naw, Honey, those people are dirt poor. We have running water and other modern conveniences."

"I'm going to make us rich one day, Mama, you just wait and see. I'm gonna buy you a real big house."

"And, where are you going to get all this money, Baby?"

"I'mma play basketball, I don't know, God will fix it. You just wait and see."

"Shhhh, be quiet, people are trying to watch the movie."

~~~

BACK TO:

Meanwhile back at the crime scene in the motel room, forensics is checking for fingerprints, detectives are scanning for evidence; photographers are shooting the layout, etc., Detectives Bud Davis and Matt Cleaver compare notes. "What do you make of it, Matt?"

"The Captain questioned one of the girls who say she hid in the bathroom when the shooting started. She didn't see much.

She says she heard somebody say, "The bitch done shot me." We followed a blood trail down the hall to the elevator and out to the back parking lot. One of the motel's guests stated that he saw three male blacks get in an early model Chevrolet and speed away. Only identifying description of the car is that is was orange and had gold rims. He couldn't make out the license plate. We got all the nearby hospitals on alert. One of the girls had a gun in her hand with six live rounds left. They took her to the hospital unconscious. She should pull through."

"Let's hope so, at least enough to be questioned. What's with this paint on their faces?"

"The girl in the bathroom says they were all just tripping."

"Tripping…on what? Drugs?"

"Could be…but, I don't know."

"These fucking niggers…they bring that jungle shit to our town…can't play a basketball game without killing each other."

"Don't go there, Bud, kids are killing kids everywhere now…killing adults too…Those trench coats boys out west, who shot up that high school, would you call them niggers? It ain't racial no more. It looks like more of a generational thing."

~~~

CHARLENE WARE

I am Carla's mother. I am sprawled on the ground in an open field around the corner from my house, staring at the moon—frantically knocking on heaven's door. As I lay dying in the outdoors, the road map of my life flashes before me.

Every choice I made, every step, every detour, every crossroad that I stood before scans in pale vision like an instant replay up to the point where I choose to light up one more time.

When I heard the news about Carla, my nerves went straight to the curve. I just had to have something to calm me. I cried, "Oh! Lord!" but He didn't answer.

I should have waited for Him to help me. He always hear my cry. He may not come when I want Him, but He's always right on time. I promised the Lord and myself two weeks ago that I was going to quit smoking and I was doing fine, until the news come over the TV about Carla and the basketball team.

Look at me; for the love of a rock, not the rock that Jesus built his church on, but a rock of crack cocaine, I lit up that bump with a straight shooter and I shot my life to the gutter. I said I was just going to try one hit. I end up trying to smoke three hundred dollars worth of crack. I done smoked up the rent money—now my lease on life is up.

When that sudden pain hit my heart, I thought I'd die right there on the spot, it was hurting so bad. I knew this was it. I said, "Lord, please don't let me die coup up in that house; don't have my baby find me stinky days later." I had to have some fresh air, some wide opened space. It was as if evil was all around me and I couldn't breathe. Somehow, I found the strength to get out of there as fast as I could—thank you Jesus! I can see my face above the clouds; I can rest in peace. Now, I know I am going to be with my Lord. My sins are forgiven, all of my shortcomings, I just hope my baby, can forgive me, too.

~~~

CARLA

I am lying up in the hospital with my knee busted from that bullet—another slug is near my spine. The doctors say it's too risky to operate. I may be paralyzed, so they decided to let me live with it inside my body. Coach brought the team by to visit this evening, which made me feel good. Then they told me Caesar took a bullet and she died on the scene. I feel so awful, Caesar of all people. Mostly, I feel bad because I can't play tonight. The team says they are going to win for Caesar and me. The cops have already been here and questioned me about the gun I had. I told them one of the dudes dropped it on the floor and I picked it up and started shooting back. G.G. should've come with the truth, but since she didn't, I just couldn't bring myself to snitch. I called my mama this morning to tell her not to worry, but she didn't answer the phone. I wonder why. She didn't go to work today, either.

I think about Eddie too, I know he's going to be mad. He's going to want to hurt somebody—maybe kill'em. I have seen the way he look at me sometimes…not as an athlete but as a piece of ass ready to be plucked like a ripe grape. I don't know, maybe those foul thoughts are in my own mind. I just feel like he's not going to want to have anything else to do with me 'cause I can't play basketball no more.

~~~

The Purple Tigers' girls' basketball team were gallant in a losing effort. They loose by only five points. With Carla out, and no post player to replace Doc, when she fouled out with seven minutes left in the game, the replacements just could not match up with the winning team's best. The best part of the game was when the girls came out of the locker room after the warm-up before the start of the game. They all had painted their faces with the team's colors in honor of Caesar and Carla. It must have been an awesome sight for the stunned crowd seeing them standing together facing the flag with the National Anthem playing. They delayed the game more than usual until the girls went back in the dressing room to clean their faces.

~~~

JUNIOR

I am Eddie Jenkins, Jr. I am Pops only son, his only child I know of. You never know about Pops. Mama says he was supposed to be a lightweight player hustler or something back in the 70's. Mom is always putting him down about how he's no good and don't care nothing about me, but I can't tell. He bought me a car and has always given me money even when he was paying child support. He may have sowed some wild oats somewhere, but I don't know nothing about it.

I go work with him sometimes just to kick it with him. He spits a lot of knowledge my way. But he wants me to be something that I am not. I am no college nigga. I don't have nothing against people who take that route, but for me it's a waste of time. I'm trying to get paid, now. I got a plan. Get the money—I can hire brains to run my shit. In this country it's all about the money. People don't give a rat's ass where your money comes from as long as you don't get caught.

Pops tell me that I am poisoning my own people when I sell dope. But if I don't do it somebody is going to sell it to them. I work with Pops and I make about a hundred dollars a day. I go stand on the corner and slang a few rocks and I make eight hundred dollars. You do the math. I don't have to work half as hard in the streets than I do when I am working with Pops.

Only risk is the police and the gang bangers who think they own this turf. Nobody tells me where I can and can't post up. I'm bout my business.

Them niggaz can taste bullets just like I can. It's whatever, whatever; I ain't never scared. I am going to get banked up, cut me some rap songs, get a record deal and it's going to be on. Pops tells me that I can take over his business one day. He tells me that if anything ever happens to him, I can go to a certain place and get the map to his money and the keys to all of his safe deposit boxes. I like being around him, he keeps me in check. But, I don't think he's being all the way real with me. I need for him to sprinkle some of that street knowledge my way. But, he won't ever go there. He thinks I am pretending and fooling myself, but I am going to show him. I am my own man.

~~~

CARLA

It is Friday, the 13th; it has been five weeks since we buried mama. I am staying with my Auntee Shirley right now. The hard cast has come off my knee and I start rehab Monday. Mama didn't have insurance, Eddie paid for everything. His actions caused a rift between mama's family and my daddy; he just couldn't understand why Eddie would do something like that. They say the casket itself cost five thousand dollars. He even gave me a thousand dollars; told me to keep it a secret, and told me that if I ever needed anything that he would be there. That's love; I don't care what nobody says.

~~~

EDDIE

A knock on my door interrupts my chef act. I am preparing a turkey salad to eat with the onion soup that's heating on the stove. When I open the door, Carla stands there; she looks at me with those big probing eyes. A hint of a smile tries to come out on her face, but her sorrow won't allow it.

"Come in Baby Girl, what that's you got in that bag?"

"Some new Jordans. I went to the mall today. I saw your car, so I had my roadie drop me off. I'm sorry if I disturbed you. I would've paged you in advance but…"

"Don't worry about it. No sweat, I'm glad you stopped by. Now, I won't have to eat alone. You just in time for dinner."

"Whatya eating?"

"Soup and salad. Got to watch what I eat at this stage of the game. You hungry?"

"No, I ate at Piccadilly's. I don't mind something to drink, though."

I tell her there is juice and water in the fridg. Carla's never stopped by my house without calling. I don't want to speculate, so I keep the conversation going.

"How much you pay for your shoes?"

"One hundred and thirty dollars…I got 'em on sale."

I almost cursed out loud when she told me that. My thoughts tell me Jordan's shit is the consummate rip-off of our kid's money and intelligence. Then I remember that shopping is the best cure for a depressed woman. So, I swallow my outburst. But that kind of money for some tennis shoes, goddamn—Mike, you ain't got no mercy on a nigger's ass.

"I see you got your cast off. How does your knee feel?"

"It's still stiff. This knee brace gives me good support. I had to see how good I could walk without those crutches."

"Well, not good."

"Uh?"

"That adverb you used in that sentence about seeing how *good* you could walk…*well* is better usage."

"Okay Dokey, Mr. Educational…"

Carla goes into the fridge and pours herself a glass of apple juice. Then she mosey on over the kitchen counter where I'm putting the finishing touches on my salad, and starts cutting small pieces of cheese to place with Ritz crackers. I tell her to wash her hands, first. She still has her backpack on and I suggest that she take it off and make herself more comfortable. When we make our way over to the table to sit down and eat, I stop in the middle of my first bite, because she pauses for a moment, bow her head, and say a silent prayer to bless her food.

"You be careful and take it slow when you rehabbing that knee. You are going to become quicker and stronger than you were before, because now, you'll be focused."

"I'm not even thinking about basketball that much anymore. When mama died, that just killed it for me. I was playing it mostly for her."

"That's ludicrous, Carla. What about yourself? You got to live for you, now. I know that you made your mother proud and everything, but I thought that you loved the game."

"I do, well I did, but I love my mama more."

"What is that suppose to mean? Sure, you love your mama more, but Charlene is gone now. Basketball is still here. That's your future—it is our future."

"I wanted to make it to the league for her. I wanted to take care of her, so she wouldn't be worried no more and stuff. Why didn't you come to the funeral?"

I don't know how to answer. Then Carla starts making one of those ugly faces and tears start coming out of her eyes. I'm still lost for words, her boo hooing is spoiling my appetite. I get up from my chair, go over to her side of the table, and put my arm around her. I tell her everything is going to be all right…that it is normal for her to grieve, and to go on and get it out of her system. What did I say that for?

She let it all hang out, snot running, wailing as if Charlene just died a minute ago. She stands up and puts her head on my shoulder. We make our way to the sofa and sit down. I'm telling her it's going to be all right. Don't worry about a thing; let's be happy, we still have each other. My tee shirt is wringing wet with her tears. I don't care. We just hold on to each other like our lives depend on it.

After a while, Carla gets up and goes to the bathroom in the hallway. She comes out with tissue blowing her nose and tells me that I am out of toilet paper. Then she says,

"Let's play PlayStation…NBA Live, I got Indiana."

I tell her I don't know how to play computerized sports games and that I am low-tech, I wouldn't be any competition. Still, Carla wouldn't let me get off. She tells me to quit being a fuddy dud and that she would show me how to work the joystick. I pick the Lakers. She beats me to a pulp game after game and she loves every minute of it. It is so funny to her watching me fumble around trying to figure out the right buttons to push. Finally, I get in sync, I learn my players and what they can and can't do. I beat her with a buzzer beater.

"Yeah, Yeah, you can't keep an old dog down. Every dog has its day, an old dog has two."

"I beat you seven games. Seven to one, you got lucky. Let's play again."

"Naw, I'm quitting while I am ahead. There's always next year."

"Quitter. What time is it? I got to call my roadie and tell her to come pick me up. I am supposed to spend the night over her house."

Carla's friend is not at home, she's not answering her cell phone, and it is a quarter to midnight. I tell her that I am going for a walk and for her to make sure she locks the door when she leaves. The truth of the matter, I need some air and distance from her. She's becoming a distraction from the state of mind I need to be in my line of work. I grab a coat from the closet and head out into the misty cool night.

Before I leave, I pick up the envelope off the table from the DNA agency, still unopened and place it in my coat pocket. While I'm walking, I tell myself to open it. But something asks me what difference does it make? Either I accept her as my daughter or I don't.

~~~

When I get back to the house, Carla is asleep on the couch, with her t-shirt and panties on—pink panties at that. I would have bet my last dollar that she would be wearing men's boxers. I turn off the television, get a blanket to cover her, and go to the bathroom in my bedroom to run some hot water in the bathtub. My hemorrhoids are burning—I need to soak ass. In the steamy water, I take a Tom Clancy book that I have been reading seems like forever. His espionage shit is boring but it is detailed and interesting. An hour passes, before I plod through five chapters and doze off to sleep.

The sound of the toilet seat dropping jolts me awake. It's Carla...she's sitting there urinating. We both are surprised or we at least pretend that we are. "Why didn't you use the bathroom in the hallway?" I ask.

"There was no toilet paper in there. I didn't think you were home. I peeped in your bedroom and didn't see anyone, so I came on in the bathroom. I'm sorry."

Caught, sprawled, genitals exposed, I wonder what she is thinking as I sit up and try to cover up with the few suds that are left in the bathtub.

~~~

CARLA

When I saw Eddie naked, my mind flashed back to Doc's story about Coach Dawson's wrinkled up shit. Only thing, Eddie's thang's is a whopper and almost straight as an arrow except it curves at the end and looks hard as steel. My pussy feels magnetized. I have dreaded this moment and starved for it at the same time. I know mama and Eddie had sex because she told me he was her first. I feel like I want to violate her because she violated me when she overdosed on that crack. It feels awkward wiping my coochie in front of him, but really, I don't care. I feel like I want to go out like a crazy bitch, too. "Can I get in the water with you?"

~~~

"Have some self-control, some scruples, nigger," I tell myself. But my silence answers Carla's question and she steps out of her panties and lifts her t-shirt over her head, then climb in between my legs. My semi-stiffness hardens until it clots against her spine as she lies back against my chest. I place Clancy's book on the floor, put my arms around her trimmed waist, and stroke her flat stomach and pubic hairs with tenderness.

I began to rationalize with Bible logic: Abraham's wife, Sarah, sent their daughter to sleep with him for her to conceive because she believed that she was too old to have a son for their heir. But this ain't Biblical, this ain't logical, it is diabolical and I still have a chance to stop this train to damnation.

I hear a voice, *"You didn't open that envelope, you don't know whether she's your daughter or not?"*

~~~

CARLA

Me and Eddie have been seeing each other intimately now for almost two months. He's great in the sack, compared to what or who, I don't know, yet, still I feel guilty. I am depressed about mama. At first I thought having sex with Eddie was getting back at my mama, but now I realized that I violated myself. I am depressed about having sex with somebody old enough to be my daddy, even my granddaddy.

I feel real bad because just like I watched my mama fuck herself sucking on that glass dick, then scrape it for crack residue; I have allowed myself to be fucked by her leftovers, too. Now, Eddie tells me that we have gone too far. Tell me something I don't know. He says that we need to chill, that we are headed for a collision. I agree with him, but I don't want to lose him, either. I don't know what to do.

~~~

EDDIE

I still haven't opened the DNA results. I am afraid to open the envelope, afraid that it will reveal the real monster that I have become, afraid that I have reveled in the destruction of the innocence of my own child. I tell myself that the god of youth is the true destroyer. Not me. That god taunts us and dares us to hold on to it. Then flees our every attempt, everyday, yet we vainly race, walk and finally crawl lower than whale shit to the bottom of the sea in search of its buried treasure until we give death the victory.

We all want to recapture the times, when we were young, when our limbs never seemed to tire. Our bodies ache for those times when the wind and we were one because all of our cares were cast unto it. We exchange our souls for a moment's illusion of pleasure, to bath in a mirage fountain of youth's treasure, and still we ask, "Is it worth it?"

~~~

CARLA

Today is Sunday and I want to go to the church me and mama use to attend. It has been a while since I last saw Eddie. Lately, my virginity has been caste into pure lust. I'm letting girls chew like goats on Billie now and I am enjoying the hell out of it.

I go into the church's foyer and listen to the singing. When the choir finishes, the preacher will start his sermon. I know the routine, mama and me came here every Sunday for some years until she got sick. When the song, *Peace Be Still* is finished, the ushers open the doors for the people to seat themselves in the congregation. I walk to the front of the pews and face all the people.

"I just want to ask everybody to pray for me," I say loud as I could. Then I walk back out into the foyer. I take a pistol from my waist that's under my shirt. I stole it at Eddie's crib that night…talking about going out with a bang! You-n-know?

EDDIE

The moment I got the news that Carla had shot herself in church, I immediately went and opened the letter from the DNA people. When I read it, I knew that this was a great day for dying. I strapped on my bulletproof vest, gathered every piece of arsenal I could carry and drove to the corner where the Vice Rulers' gang members post up. I had already done recon on them after the shooting at the state tournament. I felt like Charles Bronson, in that vigilante movie, only thing, he operated at night, for me and my pay back, it was broad daylight.

I don't give a fuck who sees me. In fact, I want this day to go down in the hood's history as a day of infamy. I want to make an open statement that Crazy Eddie shot every dope dealer and gang member he could on the corner on this day.

I wallow into a Sylvia Platt verse: *"Hear God, Hear Lucifer, beware, beware, from the ash I rise to eat men like air."*

First, I go into the Johnnie's Pool Hall. My stealthy eyes scope the place like it is a virtual reality game. I see Rat and Hard Times, two old fools I use to hang out on the corner with in bygone days. I scream, "Death to the dope pusher, death to the gang bangers, death to the wannabes, death to the busters!"

All the time I am firing my AK selectively like forty going north. People are screaming, running, and dropping like flies. Old man Johnnie ducks behind his bulletproof glass shielded counter. I know that he keeps a shotgun in back; I am on guard for him to point it at me.

Instead, he's hollering, "Eddie take it easy. Respect my place, man. What's wrong wit ya?"

Rat and Hard Times freeze like a couple of Ice Berg Slims. Their eyes beg me to send a few bullets their way with their names craved on them to take them any place other than the one they're living in; but I don't oblige. After no one is standing but Johnnie, the two gutter rat junkies and me, I proceed outside, looking for more beef to slaughter.

When I step outside, it is like a shoot out at the OK Corral, because the Vice Rulers ain't going. Two young gangstas run towards me firing at random. I'm hit three times in the chest before I hit the ground. The vest stops the slugs' penetration, and I roll over with the bitch and answer both of them deadly.

Three or four more hide behind cars, trees, and anything for cover. Another one grabs a ghetto mother walking with her infant baby by her hair and using her as a shield; he fires his gun like a blind fool shattering glass in storefronts all around me. I take dead aim, and shoot the woman in the leg. She falls to the ground screaming, crawling and reaching for her snotty nosed squealer.

Now exposed, I swing my sawed-off shotgun around from my shoulder and its accuracy tears a hole in the shooter's guts. He stands in shock, holding his intestines in his hands, and then he fall face down in the street. I swing the shotgun back on my shoulder reloading with my left hand blasting away with the bitch in my right. I break her down, reloading her while walking towards the three taking cover behind a car and some trees.

All but one of them takes to flight. The brave one walks toward me like a civil war trench soldier, holding his pistol sideways, and firing for his life. I stand to the side like a dueling aristocrat, take aim, and fire the bitch, hitting him right between the eyes. I am the last man standing.

As I walk to my truck to get out of Dodge, Granville Chatman, a lost dope fiend, who played football with me, walks up to me like death on a stick and asks to let him hold two dollars. The gall of the disrespectful louse to approach a soldier under duress with this kind of bullshit makes me want to take him out of his misery. I extend him mercy, though, and hand him a hundred-dollar bill, along with a silent prayer that he go and smoke himself to death.

Then I get in my truck and speed home. Once again, I have immersed and wallowed in the bloody sweetness of revenge. Only this time, I know that the police will be calling on me as soon as they piece the story together.

I'm sitting at home, now watching the DNA letter burn after I put a match to it. I am thinking that I'm the scourge of the earth. Any man that's done what I did is lower than a dog, the lowest of the lowest. I wish I could be tied to a whipping post, flogged ass-hole naked with a barbwire laced whip, and then left in the desert for the buzzards to feast off.

I'm *thinking* of these creative ways to punish myself to death…for being weak weak to the flesh. I am *thinking* of another Platt quote, *"Like everything else, dying is an art."*

Maybe, I should wait until the cops get here and kill all I can before they give me what I got coming. A cop suicide would be punking out; I think. I decide against it; the cops would just be doing their job. I would just be another crazy nigger with a gun that needed killing.

Perhaps, I should just pick up the bitch and do the honorable thing. However, I con myself that I am a believer…believers don't commit suicide because we are afraid we will go to hell. I feel like a coward because I'm knowing full well that I am more of an atheist than any thing else. I'm scared to roll the dice and not believe, suppose there is a God—I'm up shit creek when I die. I don't agree with atheist shit either…they make a religion out of trying to prove that there is no God.

Then I think about that preppy pervert in the book, *The Catcher in the Rye*, you know, he raised an interesting question about Judas committing suicide. He was willing to bet a thousand bucks that Jesus didn't let Judas go to hell. Forgiving as Jesus was, you know that kid might be right.

In my opinion, in a way, Jesus committed suicide. When you go up in a place knowing that you are going to be killed, to me that's a death wish, it's just like suicide. It's like those suicide bombers in a way. People will argue that Jesus was doing God's will and that he died for you and me, but that's the same thing those Palestinians buy into when they strap up with those bombs and blow themselves up trying to kill a Jew in the name of Holy War.

That's what those Japanese pilots believed when they dove their planes into those ships at Pearl Harbor. Whose to say that they were not doing God's will? Who's to say that they were not dying for their people, freedom and the greater good?

I start humming that Neil Diamond song, *I'm a Believer*, I look in the mirror, then I sing aloud, *"Then I saw her face, now I'm a believer, not a trace, of doubt in my heart, I'm in love, oooh, I'm a believer, I couldn't leave her if I tried."*

I catch myself and stop enjoying my Tom Foolery. I open Rainer Rilke's book lying on the end table beside my bed, "Poems from the Book of Hours." I sit on the bed, thumb through it, stop at one of my favorite poems, and start reciting it:

Put out my eyes and I can see you still

Slam my ears too, and I can hear you yet;
and without any feet can go to you;
and tongeless, I can conjure you at will,
Break off my arms; I shall take hold of you
and grasp you with my heart as with a hand;
arrest my heart, my brain will beat as true;
and if you set this brain of mine afire,
then on my blood I yet will carry you.

I feel brave now; I ask myself if I could write like that…words to bleed by. I chuckle to myself when I muse over the thought, "Will I bleed purple?"

I pick up the bitch and flip open her chamber. She's empty. I place one bullet in her and spin her around until she stops. I place her barrel to my head. Russian Roulette would be a fun way to go out I think. I could look in the mirror and study my face, check my fear factor, enjoy the rush, the index of relief and pain every time my brain was left in tact after each click of her trigger…I wonder…will I punk out?

First, I got to write those words. I go into my den and sit at the table. A fly buzzes at my ear. I swat at it with the bitch. I repeat aloud and old traditional piece that I haven't heard since I was a teenager. "*Niggers and flies I do despise. The more I see niggers, the more I like flies.*"

The fly, also, makes me remember a line in one of Yusef Komunyakaa's poems, "Ode to the Maggot." I think it goes something like, "*Little Master of the earth, no one gets to heaven without going through you first.*"

I think about when I die, maybe the earth will capitalize on it, nourish itself and fulfill its nature. I hear the sounds of sirens from police cars approaching from a distance. I ponder what seems like an eternity…Finally, at the eleventh hour, I scribble as legible as I can on a sheet of paper. *Kiss my black ass!*

~~~

GANGSTA GIRL

I am living in North Carolina now, except for the people being country as hell, it's all right. My mama made me move with her brother's family after I told her about Yo Dog and me and the Vice Rulers.

Sometimes, I feel sort of like a snitch. I ratted on my Boo and left Carla hanging. I wonder is she mad at me. True to what Yo Dog said, my mama went straight to the police. The police didn't arrest any of the KFL, but they rounded up five Vice Rulers and charged them with Caesar's murder and the hotel shooting. For that, I feel a little better.

I am trying to rediscover and reinvent myself. I have been studying more trying to forget my past. I find that I actually enjoy school, the newfound attention that I get for making good grades. I even took the SAT, I do not have my scores back yet, but I feel like I aced that test. I think about Carla working those puzzles all the time. I think about how I whored myself out and let those trifling niggazz run a train on me to join their gang. I think about Yo Dog and I wonder did he really love me or was he just using me...Mostly, I am just glad to be alive. Can you imagine, me, G.G., going to college?

~~~